TIANA

AN URBAN FANTASY

WAYWARD MAGE
BOOK FOUR

ANN GIMPEL

CONTENTS

TIANA
WAYWARD MAGE BOOK FOUR

An Urban Fantasy

By
Ann Gimpel

Tumble off reality's edge into a dangerous world fueled by lore and magic

Copyright Page

BOOK DESCRIPTION: TIANA

I need more time to train Tiana, but our enemies won't wait for the young Sidhe Queen to embrace her full power.

At the drop of a hat—seemingly—I became a mother. Not that I'd ever considered the possibility of parenthood. If I had, whatever I came up with would have been far off the mark.

Tiana had opinions before she was born. Ones she was vocal about.

She inherited my affinity for animals, Blake's wings, and his Sidhe royal lineage. In Underhill, they hail her as their queen, which has made raising her far more difficult. If one of us says no, she runs to her bevy of honorary aunts and uncles, one of whom is sure to indulge her.

Between Tiana's magic and her position in Sidhe society, I assumed she'd be a target from the moment of her birth.

Somehow, a dozen years have passed. I've often let my guard down—and kicked myself for my lack of vigilance.

Steeped in magic, my wild child gets lost in the moment. I need a few more years to entrain her power. But if I know that, so do our enemies. They will come for her.

When it happens, we must be ready. All of us.

Reader Note: If you enjoy urban fantasy with Celtic goddesses, unicorns, Sidhe, Cailleach, and a magical owl this story is for you. It's the 5th book in the Wayward Mage series. For the best reading experience, start with the #free prequel, *Hands of Fate*.

BOOKS IN THE WAYWARD MAGE SERIES

Hands of Fate (a novella)

Jinxed

Hunted

Salvaged

Tiana

CHAPTER 1
ABRIA

Twelve years after the end of Salvaged, the previous book in this series.

I'VE GOTTEN to know Underhill well since I took up residence here. Or maybe the magical land has gotten to know me. These kinds of things flow both ways. It took me a decade to finally let my flat in Nairn go. Blake was infinitely patient. He said I could keep it forever if it made me feel more secure, but I tired of adopting a glamour to make me appear as if I'd aged whenever I visited the place.

Since my sojourns—at least to my old flat—grew progressively fewer, I finally gave notice. My landlord was sorry to see me go. Of course, he was. I was likely one of a handful of long-term tenants who always paid the rent on time.

A sharp knock at the door was followed by it slamming against the stops as someone shoved it open. Irritation blazed a trail through me. Blake may head the Sidhe, but they afforded him little respect and less than no privacy.

I was dressed this time, a plus. Today's choice was a flowing silk skirt in muted teal and violet tones. I'd layered a white woolen tunic over it and donned sturdy brown leather boots. I've learned to put on the day's clothing the minute I waken, and I'd been up for a couple of hours.

So much for my leisurely tea-and-biscuit breakfast while I worked my way through a new scroll Blake had unearthed about my specific type of magic.

On my feet, I strode from the kitchen. Before I reached the living room, Breanne met me with Tiana in tow. The Sidhe warrior is as broad as she is tall. Her considerable bulk quivered with outrage, making the circle of white curls around her head bounce. Gray eyes zeroed in on me.

"Do you know where I found *your* daughter?" she demanded.

Rather than falling for the bait, I stared pointedly at Tiana. She glared back, defiance dripping from every cell. "You were supposed to meet Kirwan in the library for your studies," I noted.

"Ha!" Breanne snorted. "He alerted me she never showed, so I hunted her down."

Breath hissed through my clenched teeth. Why in the hell hadn't Kirwan told me Tiana was missing? How many years would it take before I was more than "the mage married to Blake"? Or Elwyn as many of his subjects preferred to call him.

"Do you have anything to say?" I asked my daughter.

A mulish expression marred her features, and she fluffed her wings preparatory to spreading them and flying away. I dropped a magical lasso over her black and indigo appendages and said, "You are not leaving."

"But I wasn't done," she whined.

Fuckity fuck. "Done with what?" I asked both of them.

"I found her in a wolf's den," Breanne growled. "Took gobs of magic to extricate her. Momma wolf wanted to rip into me."

Alarm bells ran down my back. "You didn't hurt her—"

Breanne cut me off midsentence and stabbed a beefy index finger dead center in my chest. "Of course, not. Sidhe are sworn to do no harm to the natural world. But today is a prime example of why Tiana lacks self-discipline. You taught her your magic first, rather than ours."

We'd had this discussion before—many times. I'd be damned if I'd argue with another mage in front of my child.

I latched onto Tiana's gaze. It was like looking at a miniature replica of me. She has the same long red hair, the same clear green eyes. I see Blake in her pronounced cheekbones and square chin, but she has my forehead. Womanhood is a ways distant yet.

Thank all the goddesses who've ever walked any world. Hormones will complicate everything. Today, she was in a wolf's den. Tomorrow, I might find her entertaining the Sidhe youth who trail after her like she's a bitch in heat. Except "youth" is a misnomer. The next youngest Sidhe had to top 150 years. It didn't stop them from viewing my daughter as a prime target for sex the moment her moon blood began to flow.

I pushed *that* thought aside. Sex might be a problem, but it wasn't today's issue.

I dropped a hand on my daughter's shoulder. "Go to your room. Remain there until I come to escort you to Kiran's quarters."

"But I hate my lessons. They're stupid." She stamped a foot.

"Not negotiable. Go now." I added a magical push.

So did Breanne. Still grumbling, Tiana stomped toward the hall leading to her sleeping chambers. Her wings were still hobbled, and I'd keep them that way for a while.

To be on the safe side, I shut the front door and sealed it against her leaving. Even absent wings, she could leverage teleport magic, so I closed off her room as well.

"You have to keep a closer eye on her—" Breanne sputtered.

I laid a finger over my lips. "Feel like a cup of tea?" I asked.

A surprised expression raised Breanne's white brows. When she nodded, I beckoned and led the way back to the kitchen. Once we were seated over mugs of fragrant mint and rosemary tea fortified with mead, I dropped a sound shield over us.

"The child has ears like a lynx," I said, exhaling loudly.

"If I wouldn't have found her, goddess knows what might have happened," Breanne muttered.

I trod carefully. The entire wolf pack would have laid

down their lives for Tiana, but this wasn't the time to mention it. "I appreciate you looking out for her—" I began.

"Someone has to," she inserted acidly.

So much for trying to be nice. My temper has never been my best asset, and I slapped a hand on the tabletop. "She has to develop common sense. She can't do that if I'm constantly riding herd on her."

"Doesn't appear to be working very well," Breanne observed.

I wanted to strangle her. Instead, I agreed, "It could be working better. And it would if the rest of you simply asked her if she'd run this, that, or the other thing past either Blake or me. If she lies, you'll know. If she says no, we're as close as mind speech. Ask us if she's allowed out of Underhill on her own. Or whatever she claims she has a right to do. We'll set you straight."

"She said you told her it was okay for her to visit the wolf den." Breanne glanced upward as if requesting divine intervention. "There are new pups. They fascinate her. When I arrived, she was mind-linking with them and suggesting they'd grow up to include her in their pack."

Like many of Tiana's assertions, this one held elements of truth. "I did tell her she could visit—so long as Blake or I went with her. By default, she's part of every animal pack, group, murder, flock. You name it."

"I see," Breanne muttered.

"As for the other part," I plowed on, "the one about her learning my side of magic before the Sidhe side. It's not true. Sidhe magic is complex, more difficult to entrain. Like most children, she picked the simple path, and since animals follow her as if she's the Pied Piper—"

"The who?"

"Never mind. It's a human fable about a boy with a magical pipe."

"I see."

She didn't, since she didn't know the tale, but it wasn't critical. "In any event, what child isn't fascinated by animals? They flock to her the same way they were drawn to me. Blake and I view it as harmless."

"Hmph. It is so long as she remains within Underhill's protections."

Finally, a point we agreed on. "Yes. True." I pressed my lips together. "Do you think she might do better with a different tutor?"

I expected outrage, but Breanne surprised me. "I've wondered the same. Kirwan was a solid choice for the odd youth we've produced, but he is getting on, and he's strict."

"Tiana needs strict," I mumbled.

"The way she behaves, she's a prime target." Breanne lowered her voice.

"Have you heard anything?" I demanded. Since I was still a second-class citizen in Sidhe-land, I wasn't privy to much news unless Blake chose to share.

Breanne shook her head. "All is quiet. Too quiet, if you ask me. In a few more years, Tiana will come into her full magic. No one will want to tangle with her then."

Our enemies had misjudged me—and rather badly. They could easily do the same with someone they considered a mere child, but I didn't give voice to that thought because it rattled me.

"Do you still post spies?" I asked.

Another surprised expression. "Doesn't Blake talk with you?"

I fought the same irritation that cropped up whenever the Sidhe closed ranks leaving me on the outside. "Sure, but not about everything."

"Aye, we have spies, but they can scarcely cover every world." A hesitation before she added, "And we've had no luck posting anyone anywhere near Satan's realm."

"He wasn't who we fought last time," I reminded her.

"Others like the ancient vampire exist," she muttered darkly. "We can't keep tabs on them all."

"Don't get defensive." I set my cup down and refilled it, resettling the pot between us. She could pour her own tea if she wanted more.

"I wasn't. We need a better plan for your daughter."

"And your queen." I probably shouldn't have added that jab but couldn't help myself.

Blake chose that moment to walk into the kitchen. Because of the sound shield, I hadn't heard him enter our rooms. His mouth was moving, but of course I couldn't hear him.

No matter how many years we spend together, he still steals my breath. Tall and broad-shouldered, he has dark hair cut to shoulder level, penetrating dark eyes, to-die-for facial structure, and gorgeous black wings with jewel-toned inserts. Today he wore black linen trousers and a Western-style button down pale-blue shirt with cutouts to accommodate his wings. Shiny black loafers peeked from beneath the trouser cuffs.

I held up a finger and reeled in my spell.

"Where is Tiana?" he demanded. "Kirwan told me she's missing."

"In her room," Breanne and I said in unison.

"Why can't I sense her?"

"Because I sealed her in there," I told him and girded myself for a barrage of criticism. His baby, his princess, shouldn't be confined. Especially, not against her will.

Instead of censure, he asked, "Why?"

Breanne offered a decent encapsulation of the last hour.

He hooked a chair with his foot and plopped into it. After reaching for the teapot, he realized he didn't have a cup. I pushed mine in front of him. I was done, anyway.

"We need a better approach," he said and drained half a cup of the mead-saturated beverage.

We sure did. What we'd been doing was an abysmal failure. "Mind if I haul her in here?" I glanced from Blake to Breanne.

"Why would you do that?" Breanne looked thunderstruck.

"If she's a part of decision-making that relates to her, maybe she'll be more compliant."

"Might work," Blake said and pushed to his feet.

I waggled a finger his way. "Uh-uh. I don't want you fussing over her or her whining about how badly she's been treated."

A corner of his mouth twitched; he reclaimed his chair while mumbling, "Guilty."

Reaching with magic, I removed the barrier around her room and told her, *"You will come to the kitchen now. If you deviate, you will be very sorry."*

"Oh? What would you do to me?" It's tough to project sarcasm along with telepathy, but she managed it.

Besides hang her upside down in a cave for a hundred years? Rather than reacting to her insolence, I said, *"You have thirty seconds to get your behind in here."*

On the thirty-first, she sauntered through the kitchen doorway and stopped. I could see devious little wheels turning in her head as she made a beeline for Blake.

"Father. You're home." She tried to fling herself into his arms, but he didn't uncross them.

"I'm usually home," he commented and pointed to a fourth chair. "Sit down."

Her eyes widened. Usually Blake was the softest of soft touches.

"Don't make me tell you again." Steel sat behind his words.

Tiana walked around the table and sat in the indicated chair. She made a grab for the teapot.

"Put it down," I said. "You can have tea later, and not this batch."

"I've had mead before," she announced.

"Keep your mouth shut and listen," Breanne thundered.

Defiance bled out of Tiana's expression. She looked at the tabletop, waiting. Because I could, I delved into her thoughts and found confusion. Her take-no-prisoners attitude had always worked well for her. Why was it suddenly failing?

Breanne was glaring at Blake, urging him to take his daughter to task.

He got the picture. "Tiana, look at me," he commanded. Because his words were punctuated with compulsion, she scraped her eyes upward and met her father's gaze.

"Better," he said. "One day, you will be queen to your people. I have afforded you latitude because you're a child, but today's events convinced me your childhood should have ended long since."

"What does that mean?" she mumbled.

"For one thing, it means you will do what you're told. If you do not," he went on, "there will be consequences. Ones you find unpleasant. For starters, I will separate you from the animal mage part of your power if you ever repeat a stunt like the one you pulled today."

She was on her feet in a trice. "You can't do that," she shrilled and turned to me. "Momma. Tell him he can't do that."

I shouldn't have, but I couldn't help myself. I laughed. "You're appealing to me?" I got out between bouts of mirth. "Talk about too little and too late, child."

Anger shot from her in hazy red waves. I neglected to mention she also inherited my temper. To her credit, she didn't say anything that would have sunk her deeper into Blake's bad graces.

So far, the ley lines had yet to accept her as my spawn.

Wise of them. My bet was they were waiting for her to gain wisdom.

"From here on in," Blake was saying, "your days will be structured in the following manner. After breakfast, you will spend the morning hours with Kirwan learning about your Sidhe heritage and practicing that side of your magic."

"But he's boring," she protested.

Kirwan hustled into the kitchen on the heels of her words and shook a finger at her. "I heard that, youngling. Show some respect."

"Sorry," she mumbled.

"You can do that better," Blake told her.

Tiana got to her feet, bowed, and said, "I'm sorry. It won't happen again."

She wasn't the least bit sorry about anything beyond her freedom being curtailed, but at least she was able to pretend.

The old mage nodded. He's one of a handful who doesn't employ magic to hide his age. Wrinkles sat atop wrinkles giving him the appearance of a Shar-pei. A halo of silver hair circled his otherwise bald pate. His customary black robe was draped around his short, slight frame, and his feet were bare.

"Are you done with her?" he asked Blake.

"Not quite," Blake replied and stood to face his daughter. "Once your morning lessons are over, you will have luncheon. Then you will train with Breanne three days a week to learn how to fight."

Breanne cast a sidelong glance his way that said she'd

rather host a pack of vipers, but he was her prince, so she didn't protest.

"Two afternoons a week will be spent with your mother honing your animal mage talent. The other two afternoons will be yours to choose, but you may never leave Underhill unaccompanied."

"What happens if I do?"

Aha. There was the daughter I'd come to know all too well.

"I will send you to Caer Sidi to spend at least a year with Arianrhod."

Tiana's eyes grew round. "You wouldn't."

"Och, aye, but I would. It's one place you can't escape from."

Tiana ran her palms down her black T-shirt embossed with runes and her black leather pants. For a kid who'd never been exposed to Western culture, she sure had a Goth bent.

For once, she'd run out of words.

Blake nodded at Kirwan. "She's all yours. I expect a report on each day's progress or lack thereof."

The old mage nodded sharply, crooked a finger Tiana's way, and stomped out of the kitchen.

Tiana stared at me. "I need my wings."

"What for?" I asked her.

"Sometimes they're part of the magic he teaches."

I looked at Breanne; she shrugged. Kirwan had left. I could have employed telepathy to see if Tiana had told the truth. Instead, I decided to trust my daughter. Once I unhobbled her wings, she trotted out the door after Kirwan.

A sigh rattled through me once the front door opened and shut.

Blake closed his eyes for a moment and then sat back at the table. After finishing off the mead-tea mixture, he said, "I hated to do that, but it was necessary."

His words caught my attention. "Why?"

"There is news," he said shortly. "Fell forces are mobilizing against us."

Breanne rubbed her big hands together. "Excellent. I'll call out our platoons, field them so they can sharpen their skills."

She moved fast for someone so large. It always surprised me. On her feet, she teleported out of the room.

Blake stared after her. "She didn't even wait to hear details."

"She might not have, but I need to know," I said. My mouth was dry; my stomach curled into a knot. I'd been waiting for this moment since before Tiana's birth. Now that it was almost upon us, fear gripped me.

We'd fight, but would it be enough?

Blake got up and hauled me to my feet. He wrapped his arms around me and held on tight. The show of affection—or was it desperation—wasn't making me feel any better.

"Out with it," I said, my words muffled against his shoulder.

"Come to our room," he replied. "I can shield it better than any other."

Our apartment isn't all that big, but it took several lifetimes to cover the distance from where we'd been sitting to our bedchamber. I waited while Blake shut the door and crafted a barrier around us, wanting to know and not at the same time.

When he finally turned to me, I blew out a breath I hadn't been aware I was holding and waited to discover the shape of my worst nightmares.

CHAPTER 2
BLAKE

"The queen's birth has not passed unnoticed," one of my spies mumbled. From his expression, he'd rather throw himself on his axe than be the bearer of such unpleasant news.

"What do you mean?" I bellowed at him and one other unfortunate Sidhe, both recently returned from patrolling nearby borderworlds. Like all our field personnel, they were garbed in brown leather britches with off-white woolen tunics covering their torsos. Stout boots completed their outfits, a must on some worlds where poisonous snakes prowled. One scout had a quiver of arrows strapped across his back; the other sported a smallish axe. Mostly, weapons are for show, but they do come out to play occasionally.

Shortly after Tiana's birth, I'd commandeered a room adjacent to our traditional council chamber and turned it into an office.

Like all children, she was awake at odd hours and fussy

at others, which made it challenging to conduct business in my apartment. Since she was the first child born in Underhill in over a hundred years, we had to reacquaint ourselves with younglings and their quirks. Even I had been surprised when she flew before she walked.

Made it much harder to keep tabs on her.

"Regent?" One of my minions was apparently aware my attention had taken a wrong turn. His dark hair had been dragged into a messy queue that sat low on his neck. Circles drooped beneath his dark eyes.

I nodded crisply, made a get-on-with-it gesture with one hand, and waited.

"Do you wish us to return?" the other Sidhe inquired. As fair as his companion was dark, he had pale hair chopped to shoulder length. Ice-blue eyes reflected concern.

Mmph. They must have said something I missed. Nothing for it but to bark, "Repeat everything. Start at the beginning."

I've often believed I'm not the best person to lead the Sidhe, but no one else wants the job.

He clapped a fist over his heart, the Sidhe version of "I hear and obey," and glanced at his companion. Something passed between them. I was polite enough not to pry.

"We were in the eastern quadrant," the first Sidhe explained.

"Aye, third world in," the other added helpfully.

I raked through my memories. "Isn't that a place where there's barely a breathable atmosphere?"

"The same," the first Sidhe confirmed.

"Except it's gotten a little better," the other said.

"We were engaged in our usual rounds," Sidhe one picked up the tale, "when we heard—or rather felt—something amiss."

"We took shelter," the other piped up.

Their back-and-forth recitation was beginning to annoy me, but I should have listened more closely the first time around. Nodding encouragement, I glanced from one to the other.

"The vampiric thing is back," Sidhe one said.

"Or something very like him," Sidhe two cut in.

I frowned. "How did you know it was a vampire? Did you see fangs?"

"Not exactly," Sidhe one replied.

"He smelled like a vampire," the other explained. "But there was...more."

Oh-oh. My concern deepened. "Were you at the battle twelve years ago? If so, did either of you actually see the vampire before the ley lines absorbed him?"

Both shook their heads. I wasn't sure which thing they were answering no to, but it didn't matter. What did was they'd never laid eyes on our previous nemesis. His resurrection was unlikely, but there might be others like him.

"Anyway, another just like the first abomination walked through a gateway," Sidhe one told me.

"They greeted one another like long-lost companions," Sidhe two said.

"We'd taken pains to conceal ourselves," Sidhe one explained, "but it meant we couldn't leave without alerting them they'd been overheard."

"We were there for hours," Sidhe two complained.

"Were they hatching plans the whole time?" I asked.

Both of my men made faces and looked away. "Nay, that was only the first few minutes," Sidhe one said.

"Rest of the time, they were rutting and sharing blood. It was how we knew they were vampires." Sidhe two shook his head.

Rutting, eh? Sidhe aren't exactly prudes, but same-sex pairings fly beneath the radar. We need to faery-up and join the modern world.

"Before they had sex"—I skewered both men so they had to look at me—"what exactly did they say?"

Spots of color highlighted the first Sidhe's pale cheeks. "Mostly that time had gotten away from them. They know about our queen, that she's growing up. They alluded to a group and a plan to kidnap her."

Alarm rolled through me. "And then what?"

Despite my spell, they ripped their gazes from mine. "Not for ransom," Sidhe two mumbled.

"Do they mean to imprison her?" I asked.

"If they can't end her." Sidhe one stood straighter and tried to rake fingers through his hair but was stymied by tangles.

"Time frame?" I barked.

"We don't know," they said in unison.

"We returned as soon as we could." Sidhe two stood taller, proud of making a solid decision.

"Aye, I thought they'd never leave off with their lust." Disgust punctuated Sidhe one's words.

"Should we return, Regent?" Sidhe two asked again.

"Aye, but take others with you."

"If we do, our chances of escaping notice lessen," Sidhe one pointed out.

"If you don't," I retorted, "your chances of returning at all also lessen."

I held up a hand needing to move from reacting to thinking things through. "Go to your quarters," I said, "eat and rest. I will find you within the day and relay your next set of orders."

Two fists pounded over two hearts. As a unit, the men turned and left my office. Their information hadn't been overly helpful, but it could be the difference between us being prepared or caught flat-footed.

"There you are," Kirwan boomed and shouldered into my office. "Your spawn missed her lesson time with me today." After a pause, he added, "Again."

I got to my feet and tamped down a flood of rising worry. "Any idea where she is?"

He shook his almost-bald head. "I alerted Breanne. She's out hunting for her."

"Does Abria know?"

The ancient mage shrugged.

Worry shaded to irritation. "She is the child's mother," I reminded Kirwan. "She's also the only other one here who shares the animal mage side of Tiana's magic."

Another shrug. "If Breanne comes back empty-handed—"

"Not my point. Abria—or me—should have been your first stop, and—"

He turned on me, bristling with outrage. "If the two of you had instilled respect in Tiana, we wouldn't have this problem. Or this conversation. She would do as instructed."

Harsh words withered on my tongue. He was right. Tiana was overindulged. Many firstborns tend to be, but it was a weak excuse.

"You've made your point. Return to whatever pleases you. Once Tiana resurfaces, I'll send her your way."

Kirwan angled his head to one side. "It will be a start, but she needs to show up every day. Further, she must do her assignments and practice the skills we work on. The way things have been going, she's wasting time—hers and mine."

"Thank you. I'll take care of it."

He cracked a rueful smile. "Would that it were so simple, Elwyn. All the best to you."

On that jaunty note, he walked out of my office. I wasn't far behind him. By the time I made my way through Underhill to the rooms that have been my personal domicile since I acceded to lead the Sidhe. Tiana was there, along with an outraged Breanne and an equally unhappy Abria.

I mopped up as best I could and sent Tiana to Kirwan with threats of dire consequences if she failed to apply herself. Next, I sketched out a small bit of the information I'd recently acquired. Breanne was delighted and immediately left to wrestle the Sidhe into fighting shape.

She didn't bother to wait for details. Even the slightest breath of war got her blood pumping.

Abria followed me to our sleeping chamber. Once there, I shielded it and us before speaking. I expected her to pepper me with questions, but she was unnaturally silent. Almost as if she were clinging to these last moments before whatever came out of my mouth shattered the peace we'd both taken for granted these past dozen years.

Perhaps not taken for granted, but, as more and more time elapsed, I'd hoped we were wrong about our daughter being targeted by the darkness that walked this world and others.

"Two of our patrol returned," I began. "They stumbled on vampires talking about plans to kidnap Tiana—"

"Vampires?" Abria's voice shrilled. "But the ley lines took care of him."

"There are more than one," I reminded her.

"Pfft." She paced in a tight circle. "Of course, but why do they have to be related to the one the ley lines obliterated?"

"Maybe they aren't," I pointed out. "But Jonik and Travis overheard definite plans. Whoever is after our daughter is well aware they're running out of time and need to move quickly."

Abria perched on the edge of the bed. A furrow deepened between her russet brows. She's the most remarkable woman I've ever seen. My height with waist-length hair that's always reminded me of dragon's fire, she turns heads wherever she goes. Motherhood added softness to her lush figure, making her even more enticing.

Green eyes bored into me, mining for details I didn't possess. I turned my hands palms up. "It's all I know, but we must be more vigilant. Tiana cannot leave Underhill, whether we're with her or not."

Abria buried her head in one hand. "That will not be easy. The child is headstrong."

"Aye, and 'tis on account of us never holding her accountable. That stops today."

Abria started to laugh, not in a funny-ha-ha way. Harsh, maniacal laughter spewed from her before she got hold of herself. "Sorry," she mumbled. "It's like telling a tiger to strip off its stripes. We"—she nailed me again with her green eyes—"agreed Tiana should be raised as an independent thinker. If she is to rule the Sidhe someday, she'll need the ability to make solid decisions. You don't get there if someone is always telling you what to do."

"All true." I settled next to Abria on the bed and took one of her hands in mine. "But we missed the fine line between nurturing independence and allowing her to turn into a headstrong monster."

A muted yelp told me I'd hit a nerve. Abria would defend her daughter with every resource at her disposal. I girded myself for whatever would come next, but it never happened.

"You're right, even if it pains me to admit it," she said. "I should have told her no a million times, but she's glib, that one. Quick with promises to be better—except there's always a next time."

A heartrending sigh rattled from her.

I laced my fingers with hers. "Sidhe children are pampered. This isn't all your fault." Wisely, I decided not to relay Kirwan's criticism of our parenting—or lack thereof.

"Someone will need to keep an eye on Tiana every moment," Abria muttered. "It won't be easy."

"It might be if we tell her the truth."

Abria's brows shot skyward. "But she's too young to know someone is after her."

I leveled my gaze at her. "Is she?"

"Does it even matter?"

"What do you mean?" I asked.

"We have to leverage every resource at our disposal to protect her," Abria said. "Maybe we should send her to Arianrhod or Cailleach until we get a better handle on who's after her and how we can cut the knees out from under them."

"This time," I said softly.

Abria's shoulders slumped. She leaned into me. "This will be ongoing, won't it? Even after she ascends the throne—or whatever you call it."

"'Fraid so. Except in another dozen years, her magic will be far more robust than it is today."

"Why did this never occur to us when I ended up pregnant?" Abria shook her head. "Never mind. Her life was goddess-given. She's here for reasons I have yet to fully fathom."

I let go of her hand and wrapped an arm around her shoulders. "Aye, and so long as she is, we will defend her."

Abria sputtered and stumbled, but no words emerged. She clearly wanted to say something. "It's all right," I reassured her. "Just spit it out."

"Your people aren't all too fond of me. What makes you think they'll stand up for Tiana? If enough shit gets tossed their way, they may decide she's too much of a liability and relegate her to animal-mage land, rather like the Celts did with me."

It could happen, but I wasn't ready to go there. "Let's not borrow trouble. For now, we need to do two things."

"And they are?"

"Gather more information about what forces are marshaling against us—"

"And turn Tiana into a different child, a compliant one who respects rules." Abria muffled a snort.

"An uphill effort, to be sure, but we have no choice." I'd been thinking about Jonik and Travis and what to do next. "I'd like to go to the borderworld where my people found the vampires."

"I want to come too, but one of us has to remain with Tiana. She's such a hellion, I wouldn't want to palm her off onto anyone else." Abria paused long enough to suck in a breath. "I've got it. We can leave her with Arianrhod. Then we'll both go. Strength in numbers, plus I carry the weight —and magic—of the ley lines."

"Better check with Arianrhod," I said, not at all certain how the goddess would react to babysitting a recalcitrant not-quite-teenager.

"I'll send Hedrek." A brisk whistle followed her words. In short order, a large tawny owl with golden eyes flew right through the ward I'd built and landed on the floor in front of us.

"You two look like you just lost your closest friend," he hooted.

"Hasn't happened yet," I told the owl, "but I fear hard times are about to befall us."

"Could you ask Arianrhod if she'd be willing to keep Tiana safe for a few days?" Abria asked.

"Certainly. How many days?"

"Not more than a week," I clarified and hoped to hell I wasn't wildly off-base.

"Anything else?" Hedrek looked from one to the other of us. He's canny, and I'm certain he saw more than we'd revealed.

"Nope," Abria replied. "Thank you. We'll prepare Tiana for possible transport to Caer Sidi."

"Better you than me," the owl tweeted and was gone in a shower of golden motes of light.

"He knows her too well," I said.

"I rest my case about your people not wanting to go out of their way for a spoiled, entitled brat, even one who is slated to be their queen. Frankly, I don't blame them. Respect has to be earned, and we've done a piss poor job as parents." Abria got to her feet. "These next few weeks will be sheer hell, but we have to establish better boundaries."

"And ground rules," I agreed and stood too.

I offered her my hand, took down the warding I'd crafted around us, and led the way into Underhill. My plan was to stop in Kirwan's study, collect our daughter, and lay down the law.

"Don't be too hard on her," Abria began, and then added, "Don't mind me. She needs harsh. Our magic still trumps hers, but it won't forever. If we don't get a handle on this now, we never will."

I thought about mortal children, ones who ran away, got themselves into huge trouble, and never looked back. Not that she was mortal, but I said, "We could use Roya as a resource and living example."

Abria stopped just past the door to our rooms. "Why?"

"She sat at a nexus betwixt magic and mortals, chose badly, and paid a bitter price."

Abria nodded slowly. "Are you going to fetch her from the *Dreaming*?"

"Aye. Back very soon."

I kissed Abria, wished for ever so much more than that fleeting pressure of my lips against hers, and left. Maybe I could convince Roya to accompany Tiana to Caer Sidi.

Or not.

Roya may have lost her hands to her all-too-human faux father in the place I'd sent her as a changeling to guard a portal into Underhill, but she was Sidhe to her bones. Tiana's high-handed lack of respect would infuriate her.

Doesn't hurt to ask.

Besides, I had no idea if Arianrhod would say yes. The goddess had been insulated from the worst of my daughter's tantrums and insolence, but it wouldn't take her long to get up to speed.

One step at a time, an inner voice counseled as the soft, muted light of the *Dreaming* formed around me.

One step at a time.

CHAPTER 3
ABRIA

After breathing in the heady scents of Blake's magic—damp earth, sunbaked stone, and the brine of every ocean—I turned, intent on reentering our rooms, but cursed myself for a coward. I'd collect Tiana from Kirwan and begin what I should have done years ago. To my credit, I never had any parental role models floating about. I wasn't exactly born; the Celts created me and then dumped me in a cave.

They made certain my creature comforts were attended to, but nothing beyond. When I made good on an escape, it shocked them. Still, they didn't expend even an iota of energy hunting for me.

See what I mean about lacking parental role models? Any caregiver worth his/her salt would have chased down a runaway kid. The Celts, not so much.

"Pity party, much?" I mumbled and set a course for Kirwan's study. It was near the library. Made sense because the old mage was a veritable walking compendium of Sidhe history.

As I walked, I resurrected bits and pieces of Tiana's short life. Naturally, everyone had been smitten with the red-haired, green-eyed infant. As she'd grown, animals flocked to her just as they did to me. Somewhere between her third and fourth year, she'd discovered how simple it was to manipulate adults to meet her needs, and her engaging smile covered the worst of her sins.

At that age, they weren't all that serious, and everyone rushed to offer excuses and forgiveness.

I'd brought up the problem many times, but Blake assured me all Sidhe children were spoiled, and they grew out of the worst of their egregious behaviors. Unfortunately, Tiana's were doing nothing but getting worse.

The older she got, the more headstrong and disrespectful. I'd specifically forbidden her to visit the wolf family on her own, yet she'd done just that. My prohibition meant nothing.

The sound of raised voices reached me long before the final bend in the tunnel that would deposit me near the library.

"Get down from there this instant!" Kirwan shouted.

"Make me. You can't fly anymore. Admit it, old man."

Fuck. Fuck. Fuck.

I broke into a run, skidded around the corner and through the open library door. Kirwan was on his feet, arms raised with power arcing from his fingertips. My spawn flitted this way and that knocking down priceless books and scrolls to make a point.

Any inclination I'd had to give her a chance shattered. I shaped a magical lasso on the fly and tossed it around her wings, cinching it tight. She floundered, tried to fill in with her arms, failed, and crashed to the floor.

"Ooph." Tiana rolled to her feet cradling one arm. "You hurt me." Accusation rippled beneath the words, but I was beyond caring.

I pointed to a chair. "Sit there."

When she just stared at me, defiance oozing from every pore, I scooped her up with magic, dropped her into the chair, and added a short ley line tether to make certain she couldn't get up.

"You can't do that," she squealed, writhing against the invisible bonds holding her in place.

"Just did." Turning to Kirwan, I asked, "What happened?"

"He'll lie," Tiana announced.

"Would you like me to seal your lips as well?" I didn't bother turning to glance her way.

"You wouldn't. I'm your queen, and—"

That did it. I stomped to where I'd dropped her and thumped her hard in the breastbone with my index finger. "You will never be my queen. I am not Sidhe, or have you forgotten? In terms of everyone else, respect must be earned. The Sidhe will never accept you in any kind of leadership position unless you've proven you have what it takes to lead."

I stopped to grab a breath. "The way things are going, I'm not hopeful."

"How can I prove anything? No one lets me go anywhere you're not breathing down my neck."

"By doing what you're told." Kirwan stepped into the breach.

I shot a glance his way. "What happened before I got here?"

The old mage shrugged. "She has yet to demonstrate patience or discipline. Subjects like history and mathematics bore her."

"Mother never went to bloody school," Tiana piped up.

Yeah. Never should have told her that. "I've spent hundreds of years playing catch-up and regretting the lack of someone like Kirwan to teach me."

"Didn't get in your fucking way."

"Watch your mouth!" I put steel behind my words.

Sheesh. Was I only now in this moment seeing Tiana for who she was? A foul-mouthed brat with a total lack of regard for anyone in a position of authority?

"If you say one more word," I told her, "I will seal your mouth. Do we understand one another?"

"But—"

This time, I crafted visible power and split off a piece of the ley line holding her in her seat. Once it was free, I instructed it to cover her petal-blossom mouth. Tears welled, dripping down her fair skin.

Fake remorse wasn't going to cut it. Not anymore.

I focused on Kirwan. "You were saying?"

"Your daughter is bright, but flighty. If she were to apply herself, she could go far. As it is, self-indulgence trips her up. Because no one has ever forced her to do, well, anything beyond what she chooses, she has the attention span of a sandfly."

A muted squawk of protest wriggled past the barrier over Tiana's mouth. I felt like a shithead, but we had to establish ground rules sometime.

"She's behind in all her studies," Kirwan went on. "Not that she has classmates to use as a comparison, but I've taught generations of Sidhe youth, and all of them were light years ahead of her when they were her age."

"How should we proceed?" I asked.

"Breanne tells me enemies are lurking." At my nod, he went on, "We must send her away until we've dispatched whatever confronts us. 'Tis a sure bet, they're coming for her."

Tiana's eyes were still doing their fountain imitation, but I thought I picked up worry behind her fake tears.

"Our take too," I told him. "Hedrek is on the hunt for Arianrhod. Blake seeks Roya from the *Dreaming*."

Muted squawks grew louder. Tiana's wings were hobbled; she was tied to the chair. Still, she protested. I offered her an A for spirit and an F for brains and insight.

I turned my full attention on her. "If Arianrhod will have you, which is far from certain, you will go to Caer Sidi. If you give her even a breath of a problem, I plan to offer her carte blanche in terms of suitable consequences."

It was refreshing to have my daughter's undivided attention absent any backtalk. "Roya might accompany you. In case you don't recall, she's a changeling your father set to guard one of the entrances into Underhill. Because she didn't exactly follow instructions, she was caught up in a clan war. It's how she lost her hands."

In answer to the question I saw in Tiana's eyes about why Roya hadn't simply used magic to repair her lost appendages, I went on. "Not everything is fixable, no matter how strong one's magic is."

Because I'd been intent on Tiana, I didn't notice energy bearing down on us until Hedrek's hoot snapped my head around. The owl and Arianrhod stepped through a gash in the air.

Tall and lithe, Arianrhod wore leather garments crafted from dark-colored hide. She examined me from bi-colored eyes: one gold, the other silver. Hair like spun gold had been gathered into a bun at the nape of her neck. A bronze torc studded with turquoise circled her neck, and her hunting bow was secured across her back in a battered sheath.

The goddess arched a brow. "Motherhood wearing a bit thin, eh?"

I started to sputter that wasn't it at all, but the lie died on my lips. She'd know. Walking in on our tableau with Tiana trussed up like a Christmas hen was a dead giveaway.

With a casual wave of one hand, the goddess released Tiana's bonds.

"Finally!" The child bounded to her feet and spread her wings. "Someone understands me."

"Not so fast." Arianrhod ended up in front of Tiana. I never saw her move; she was just there.

My daughter didn't exactly fall on her knees, but she did bow low and murmur, "Thank you for freeing me. I'll be on my way now."

"I think not." Another hand wave, and Tiana froze midstep.

Arianrhod sent a sidelong glance skittering my way. "The only way I will agree to be her temporary guardian is if I have absolute sovereignty over how I manage her."

Blake strolled into the room, Roya by his side. Waiflike and thin to the point of emaciation, she was surrounded by clouds of pale red hair. Deep brown eyes sat above slanted cheekbones. Rather than her usual robes, she wore green linen trousers and a puffy white jacket. Sandals covered her feet; both arms ended in stumps where hands had once been.

"Good timing," I told them.

Roya hurried to Arianrhod and curtseyed. "Goddess. Elwyn asked if I might accompany his daughter to Caer Sidi. I am willing if you will have me."

"Good idea," Hedrek hooted.

"Why is that?" Arianrhod glared at her familiar.

Roya curtseyed again. "I made many mistakes, goddess. Perhaps ones the young queen might learn from."

Tiana would have had a snappy comeback were she not frozen in place.

Arianrhod nudged Blake. "Did you hear my conditions?"

"Aye."

"Are you in agreement?"

Because I was watching Tiana, I saw twitches—all she could manage—of outrage spilling through her.

"Of course," Blake was saying. "Full agreement. I hope she doesn't give you any trouble."

Arianrhod kicked her head back. Laughter rolled from

her. The harder she laughed, the angrier Tiana became. Her face turned brilliant red; veins in her neck and temples stood out, beating hard.

My heart ached for her. She was only a baby. My baby. My job was to nurture her, protect her…

"*Yes,*" a small voice insinuated. "*Help me, Momma.*"

Whoa. Somehow, Tiana had managed to push telepathy past Arianrhod's barriers. And not just telepathy. My money was on compulsion rippling behind the "only a baby" part of my inner dialogue.

They were getting ready to leave. I could remain silent; no one would be the wiser. I balled my hands into fists. More compulsion. Nothing wrong with Tiana's magical ability. If we couldn't shape it to perform other than subterfuge and manipulation, she'd be a prime target for damn near anyone.

Mostly because she had ultimate faith in her ability to run rings around everyone and everything.

"Wait." I held up a hand.

Arianrhod had already begun to build her journey spell. "Aye?"

"Tiana defeated part of your immobilization spell. She's been shoveling compulsion at me. And telepathy."

Blake turned an incredulous expression my way. "You must be imagining it, Abria."

"Pfft. She got to you too. You just aren't aware of it."

The goddess slung an arm around Tiana and picked her up as if she weighed nothing. "If you choose not to behave," she said, "I will suspend you upside down in my dungeon and invite a few dragon friends to mark you with their fire."

Roya took up a position on the other side of Tiana. Hedrek fluttered to my shoulders.

Arianrhod snapped her fingers at the owl. "None of that. You're coming with us."

"But I'd planned to travel with Abria to where vampires were sighted," the owl said.

"You may be able to do that. Let's get this piece of baggage home and see how many of us it takes to ride herd on her."

Kirwan had been so silent, I'd all but forgotten about him. He lumbered over to the goddess and bowed low. "If 'tisn't too much trouble, my lady, the youngster needs study time."

"Which topics?"

"History and math."

Arianrhod rolled her bi-colored eyes. "Fine. I'll scare up Gwydion. He's got the history part down cold. Hopefully"—her gaze scoured first Blake and then me—"she won't be with me long enough to delve into mathematics."

"I can help with either or both," Roya offered.

"I'll hold you to it. Ready?" Arianrhod offered a smile that was mostly teeth. In seconds, the room emptied of all but Blake, Kirwan, and me.

"I hope we did the right thing," Blake muttered.

"You did." Kirwan sounded certain. He turned his aged hands palms up. "Something had to change. Something drastic. Tiana has been on a collision course with disaster for far too long."

"Why didn't you say something?" Blake demanded.

"I tried. You're selectively blind when it comes to those you love."

I winced and mumbled, "Equally guilty." Eventually, I'd miss my daughter. At the moment, I savored being out from under the constant pressure of wondering what she was up to this time.

"I will find Breanne, see what assistance she requires," Kirwan said and left the library.

Once he was gone, I mumbled, "We didn't do our daughter any favors."

"But she'll be saddled with responsibility for the Sidhe soon enough. I wanted her to have a childhood."

"Understood." I leveled my gaze his way. "If she doesn't shape up, the leadership position will remain in your lap. I may not be Sidhe, but they won't support her in any capacity if they can't respect her."

"She's still a child—" he began, but then thought better of continuing. We'd both clung to that argument, and look where it had gotten us. Not very fucking far.

"In truth, her moon blood will flow soon. She'll be playing catch-up learning the self-discipline we should have instilled," I said.

"We can't go backward. Maybe Arianrhod will provide a solid base for our next steps with Tiana. Are you certain you want to accompany us on the vampire reconnaissance?" Blake turned to me. His features had smoothed into an unreadable mask. Probably meant he was as conflicted as I was about our failure as parents.

"Quite sure. Give me five minutes to change into something more suitable for unknown climates. Where shall I meet you?"

"The council chamber. I'll scare up Jonik and Travis."

"Deal." I sprinted down the corridor grateful to have something to do beyond worrying about how Tiana was settling in at Caer Sidi. I hadn't done all that well my first time there. Arianrhod was a dour soul, all business and no warmth, but Tiana needed someone like that. Someone she couldn't charm to do her bidding—or who'd turn a blind eye to her poor behavior.

I hurried into heavy denim trousers, a stretchy top, and a warm hooded jacket. Everything including my boots was black. As an afterthought, I gathered my long red hair into a queue and threaded it beneath my jacket. If I pulled up my hood, I could effectively hide its usual ruddy glow.

After a final look around to make certain I hadn't forgotten anything, I set a path for the council chamber. The Sidhe waiting with Blake could have been mirror image twins, one fair and the other dark. Like all Sidhe, they held an ethereal beauty that belied their efficiency as warriors.

The dark-haired one inclined his head. "I am Travis, my lady."

I bowed in return.

"And I am Jonik," the blonde informed me.

"We were in the field on the occasion of your wedding," Travis said.

"Or else, we'd have been there," Jonik cut in.

"Good to meet you." I bowed again.

Blake was apparently done with pleasantries. He swept

us all into a journey spell while muttering, "I want to get this part over with."

I wondered how he knew where to take us, but trusted we were on track. We needed to talk about what would come next for our child—except she was scarcely one at this point. It would have to wait until we were alone.

The other thing that needed to take a back seat was my burgeoning sense of guilt. I'd known since Tiana's birth she'd need to be ready for something like this, but I'd put off holding her responsible for anything. Let alone training her to be alert and on the defensive.

I'd wanted her to have the childhood that had been denied me. Understandable, maybe, but not very smart.

"Third world in, eastern quadrant?" Blake asked the other Sidhe.

"Aye, Regent," Travis said. "If I may be so bold, Jonik and I are relieved you changed your mind about bringing more troops on this venture."

Blake's reply was a noncommittal grunt.

The first part of Travis' comment explained how Blake knew where he was going. I'd visited a handful of border-worlds, but none in this region.

"Join my casting," Blake invited Travis and Jonik. "I don't want to bring us out in the middle of an enemy camp."

Visible bands of shimmery light formed between him and the other men. I felt the shift as we prepared to leave the comforting darkness surrounding us. It's hard to explain, but it's not unlike pressure changes as commercial aircraft come in to land. Not that I've ever been on one, but I've read about them.

"Abria." Blake's tone was sharp.

He didn't need to say anything further. I warded myself and gathered defensive magic, balancing it between my hands while toning down its brilliance. Speaking of which, I freed one hand long enough to toss my hood over my head.

Our landing wasn't especially elegant. We thumped down hard enough to knock the breath from me. I regrouped fast, expecting to be rushed from all sides. The old-blood smell of vampire was thick in my nostrils, but no one reacted to our presence.

My lungs burned. Precious little oxygen here. I did what I could to concentrate it before breathing it in. The ground was cracked into hundreds of tiny runnels suggesting flash floods washed through here from time to time. I couldn't smell water, but it didn't mean rain didn't fall occasionally.

Rather than brown, the dirt was a nondescript gray with black streaks.

"They were through there." Jonik pointed between two misshapen boulders.

Taking care to move silently, and still well warded, I crept forward. By the time I reached the nearest boulder, Blake had pulled ahead. His ward was sloppy, but I didn't point it out—not in front of his men.

"No one is here now," he said.

"Left recently from the stench," Travis mumbled.

Since we were here, I began a methodical transit of the small clearing in front of us in hopes of finding clues. No such luck. Not as if they used electronic tablets or spiral-bound notebooks. Or wrote in the dirt with a sharp stick.

Not much reason to waste magic on telepathy. "Where do you suppose they went?" I asked.

"Wherever it was, they left in a hurry," Blake growled.

"How can you tell?" Travis asked.

"It's daylight, not their preferred time to travel." Blake jabbed a finger at the grayish sky with a teensy sun wobbling across it.

"We could track them," Jonik suggested.

Something cold slithered down my back. We could, but it was risky. My experience with vamps is limited, but they hate being cornered. Hell, nearly everyone does.

Blake drew his brows into a thick, dark line. "I wish I'd invited Kirwan along. Vampires have a home world somewhere in this quadrant. Could be this one for all I know."

The chill that had begun in my back spread to my arms and legs. Reflexively, I sent power in a 360 degree arc checking for anything alive beyond the four of us.

And reeled it in fast but not fast enough. The peculiar feel of vampire essence sprinted toward us along with their nasty carrion smell. They cloak it when intent on luring mortals to the dinner table, but the rest of the time, it hangs around them in an unpleasant miasma.

Dried blood. Rotten blood. Rotten flesh.

Reminded me why they were called the undead. Their bodies froze in time once they were turned. Wounds never healed. Teeth and nails rotted from the inside out. The truly old ones swathed themselves in glamours. If they didn't, they'd have starved.

"*Abria!*" Blake grabbed my arm, half dragging me as he dove for an opening in the ground.

Jarik and Travis piled in on top of us. I didn't get why we weren't leaving.

Blake layered invisibility spells over us, one atop the other. I reached for the ley lines, pleasantly surprised to find their distant cousins in this remote spot. In case I needed to punch things up, I opened a channel to them.

Footsteps pounded over our hiding place, running this way and that.

"Sidhe were here," someone shouted.

Naturally, they could smell Blake and the others.

"Something else, too," another yelled.

"Find them." A third voice rang with command. "No one feeds until you do."

"But, Mingus. They left," still another voice whined.

The sharp ring of flesh against flesh suggested Mingus didn't tolerate backtalk.

We could teleport from here. Why weren't we? Sure, there'd be a burst of obvious magic, but by then we'd be gone.

Something like a rusty bayonet jabbed into our hiding place, withdrew, and jabbed downward again. Travis was on top. If they cut into him, they'd smell his blood, and the jig would be up.

The next time the stabby thing came close, I touched it with the end of a ley line. A sharp squeal made me grin.

"What is it? You sound like a scalded cat," Mingus groused.

"Nothing, boss." Guess he didn't want to admit weakness.

I waited, but no more jabs disturbed our immediate

vicinity. After a while, the footsteps moved away. So did the voices.

When they were far enough away, I risked telepathy. *"Why are we still here?"*

"We came for information," Blake explained. *"While they're busy hunting for intruders, we split up and see what we can glean by eavesdropping. Meet back here in an hour."*

One by one, we crept from our hiding place. My muscles had stiffened, but they'd survive. After making certain my concealment spell was bombproof, I set out to the north. Blake went south. The others took east and west.

After a few minutes, I came to a rough road formed by stones stuck into dirt. Which way should I go? An hour wasn't all that long, and I didn't dare risk another magical scan. My first had landed us in the current pickle. Running on instinct, I turned right and hugged the side of the road. Dwellings came into view and a city wall, gateway standing open.

Did I dare go inside? It was the most likely place to over-hear something useful. My heart pounded so hard, I felt certain nearby vampires could hear me. Or smell me.

No one batted an eyelash.

Slipping around one group and skirting another, I entered their town intent on locating handy alleyways. Out of nowhere, a bell began to toll, long, low, mournful.

Vampires rushed this way and that. At first, I assumed the bell signified something, like perhaps the close of a workday or a meal/blood announcement.

Didn't take long before I put two and two together. My presence had tripped some magical ripcord. The vampires knew someone had breached their city. A stone gate crashed down, effectively sealing off my escape route.

I could climb the wall, but not with my ward in place. Someone would spot me. I started to summon a transport spell with help from the ley lines, but then stopped cold. I was in a perfect position to hunker down and learn something. I could always flee.

Brave words.

By my count, I had maybe forty-five minutes before Blake came looking for me. Determined to make the best possible use of it, I ducked into the first building, on the prowl for information.

If they had solid plans to kidnap Tiana. I'd strip them bare, expose them to daylight, and defeat them.

When nothing of interest was in the first building, I moved on to the second.

I'd made it to what looked like a central meeting room when I heard, "Block off this one. He's in here."

He, huh? Funny how there's always the implicit assumption women are incapable of anything beyond cooking, cleaning, and having kids.

Not so funny since someone had just closed off the primary door into this place. Unlike Blake, I lack wings. Flying out an upstairs window wouldn't cut it. I could wait them out, but it was a bad idea. Blake would come hunting for me, and then he'd be trapped too.

Desperate, playing for time, I raced down an empty corridor, barricaded myself into a room, and built a spell to move me the hell out of there. I got it together, ignited it, and waited.

Nothing.

Had I missed something? Unlikely. Still, I went through every element, checking each one thoroughly.

Heavy steps plodded down the corridor.

Cornered, I reestablished my linkage with the ley lines and turned to face the door just as it slammed open. Power crackled around me, turning the air blue-white.

"Found her," a Neanderthal-appearing vamp shouted and hurried closer, fangs extended. Black hair hung down a low forehead and into dark eyes. Dressed in bloody skins he looked like a throwback to goddess only knew what.

Fury spilled through me. I channeled ley line power dead center in his chest. A burning hole appeared, drilling its way through him.

He jumped back, a shocked expression on his face.

I grinned. Energy crackled from my fingertips. "Bring it on," I told him and whoever else was close enough to listen. "Not sure if I can end your miserable undead life, but I'm sure as fuck going to try."

CHAPTER 4
TIANA

Finally, I get my own chapter. The bloody book carries my name. I'm on the cover, but it isn't a great likeness. No one listens to me. Ever. I wanted to look older. The kid on the cover could maybe have been me when I was eight. I'm taller now, and I have breasts. Well, sort of. They'll be bigger soon.

Those pithy little thoughts took place in my head.

Arianrhod, bitch of the universe, had me in a chokehold. She blunted my senses with her magic. Took me a while, but I managed to worm a hole in the crap she swathed me in.

Did Mother listen? Oh hell, no. Just adopted her "thoughtful" expression while I was carted off to a concentration camp. Yeah, learned about them when I grabbed books I was actually interested in from the library.

Kirwan has no sense of humor. None. When I'm not totally immersed in what he wants me to read, he rebukes me, grabs what I have in front of me, and hides it somewhere.

I've tried to find stuff before. Occasionally I struck gold, but not often. He's boring, but he's also smart. Pains me to admit it.

I have no idea why Mother and Father thought having me was such a grand idea. I'm a freak. Not exactly Sidhe and only the second animal mage in all of existence, Mother being the first.

I love being an animal mage. They're the only ones who welcome me, who love me. The Sidhe are a bunch of stuck-up fuckers with their heads up their asses. They look at me like an interesting piece of trash, and I hear them talk when my parents aren't around.

The odds of me ever being queen are about as good as the odds of Underhill suddenly selling out to Satan. It could happen, but it probably won't.

Want to know what I think?

Don't answer that. I'm going to tell you anyway.

Father is sick of leading the Sidhe. He never wanted the job in the first place. I've heard him say exactly that often enough. So he had me as a way to get out from under it.

He needs to think again. I'll run away before I end up tethered to Underhill for eternity leading boring meetings with boring people I can't stand. I won't do it.

My magic is growing stronger. One of these days, I'll run where they can't track me, and I'll stay gone.

Yeah. Perfect. Just need to bide my time, catch them off their guard. Might be a couple of years from now, but once

I've made good on my escape, I'm never going back. I'll gather my own group of animals, and—

The mishmash of words tumbling through me halted. It would never work. Mother could find me if I called so much as a single beetle to my side.

The specter of a lonely existence spread before me. My eyes burned, but I refused to let tears fall. They were for babies, and I was almost grown up.

The blackness around us changed to a desolate shore. Cold drilled into me. My nose burned from briny air. Where were we? Did the goddess live on this godforsaken stretch of coastline?

"I will release you because you must walk through the gateway on your own." Arianrhod shook me to punctuate her words. Hard. My teeth bounced off each other Luckily, I didn't bite my tongue in two. It was close.

Pathetically grateful to be mistress of my body once more, I looked from side to side. If a gateway was near, I couldn't pick it out. All I saw were ice-crusted boulders and wet sand. My house slippers soaked through immediately. Instinctively, I sent magic to warm my frozen toes.

It never made it. The bitch may have let me go, but she still controlled my magic.

"I said walk," Arianrhod barked. "Now."

"Which way?" I tried to sound cowed. Bet I didn't fool her. I was pissed. If I weren't worried she'd make good on her promise to hang me upside down by my wings, I'd have hauled off and slugged her.

In lieu of magic, I fluffed my wings around my body. It could have worked better. I began to shiver, wings and all.

"Why, toward the portal, child."

I peered through gray mist, couldn't see a thing, and struck out to my right hoping I'd guessed correctly. I'd die before I'd admit I couldn't sense a portal. It was magic 101. Even newborns felt drawn to their energy.

A clawlike hand closed around my upper arm, squeezing hard. "Not that way. What's wrong with you?"

Defeat swamped me. I was chilled to my bones, couldn't feel my feet. Plus I was tired, and starving. To my absolute horror, a sob burst from my constricted throat, followed by several more. I buried my head in my hands to hide my shame.

"Never mind." The hand dragged me forward. I staggered to keep from sprawling facedown in the icy sand. Hanging onto my pride no longer claimed a starring role. I'd moved to survival mode.

We shuffled to an enormous boulder that might have been shaped like a dragon. I was afraid she was going to slam me into it, but the thing opened as we came close, allowing us inside.

I was still sobbing. Snot ran down my face; I was too demoralized to wipe it off. The bitter cold receded, but I couldn't stop shivering. In a distant corner of my mind, it sank in that the goddess had let go of me.

I sank to a wretched heap on a stone floor—a warm stone floor—and hugged my arms around my knees. What was wrong with me? I hadn't cried since I was three years old.

Now I couldn't stop.

For the moment, Arianrhod was gone. Intent on escape,

I reached for my magic. I'd seen the way inside. Surely, the passage went both ways. My first effort boomeranged back and slapped me in the gut. Breath whooshed from me; I grabbed my middle and tried not to puke.

Okay, then.

If magic wasn't the ticket out of here—and mine was definitely offline—I'd walk. Determined to extricate myself from Arianrhod's clutches, I forced myself upright and turned in a slow circle. Which way had I come in?

I was in a square chamber. Everything was gray stone: walls, floor, even the ceiling. No windows. I reached for my power again and girded myself for the fallout. This time, nothing happened. Nada. Zip. Zilch. It was as if I'd never commanded power to begin with.

One door in the far wall was closed. On a whim, I walked to it and twisted the latch.

It opened.

I fell back a step. I'd expected to be locked in. Peering down a corridor lined with the same gray stone, my visual field ended with a sharp bend. It didn't require enchantment to understand this wasn't the way I'd entered Caer Sidi. We'd probably oozed through a wall, a task currently beyond me.

Was the open door a trap? If I stepped through, would I regret it? I clung to the area in front of the door as I pictured what might happen.

I'm not used to overthinking things. I do whatever I want as the mood strikes me. Over the years, I've grown adept at getting my way. All I have to do is smile pretty at Father. Mother is tougher, so I've learned to stay out of her way. Or I pass through when she's preoccupied. The only time we get along is when we're with animals.

I took another step back. Fury beat a tattoo through my veins. I refused to let this defeat me. Chin high, I marched through the door. It couldn't have been left unlatched by accident.

Arianrhod didn't seem the type to miss anything.

Wingbeats headed my way. Footsteps too, but not the goddess's distinctive tread. I stopped in my tracks, defiance forgotten. Was the promised dragon coming to flay me with fire?

Hedrek, the owl from Kirwan's study swooshed around the corner with Roya in his wake. I turned back toward the stone room, but the owl blocked my way.

"Come with me," Roya instructed.

"Why should I?"

She grabbed my arm by hooking hers around it and spun me to face her. "Because for starters, I have dry clothes laid out for you. Food and tea await as well."

"Not hungry," I lied in hopes the two of them would leave me to my misery.

Something sharp pecked my shoulder. Running on instinct, I swatted at the owl. Of course, I missed. My reward was an even harder peck.

"None of that," Hedrek hooted.

Roya still had my right arm in a death grip. Considering her slight build, she was strong. "You will come with us." Compulsion battered me. I had no magic of my own to divert it.

Suddenly, dry clothes seemed like an awesome idea. My

empty stomach rumbled at the possibility of food. I tried to curl my hands into fists; they refused to cooperate.

A battle had played out here, and I'd lost without even throwing a punch.

Shit.

I had to play along. Yeah, that's it. I'd be a model prisoner, so compliant they'd let their guard down.

And return my magic.

The second that happened, I'd be out of here so fast Hedrek's tail feathers would wither and fall out. The image amused me, but I knew better than to laugh.

Best not think, either, an inner voice cautioned. They could read my mind if they chose.

I let them herd me down the corridor we stood in, and then along several others, all the while trying to build a mental map of this place. If it was anything like Underhill, my effort was a lost cause. Magical lands shift and change to suit their fancy.

"Here we go," Roya's voice echoed with false cheer as she guided me into a room. "We'll give you a spot of privacy to change out of your wet garments."

The door swung shut, and I was alone. For the moment.

I shucked my soaked trousers, tunic, and house slippers, looked at them on the floor, and hung the first two items on hooks. Probably no servants here to wait on me. Soft fuzzy black woolen pants, a matching top, shoes, and socks had been stacked nearby. I pulled them on, grateful for their warmth.

The heady scent of tea and a pungent cheese drew me to a small table. I plopped into a chair and dug in. No point starving myself. I'd become weak and less able to wield my power once it was restored.

What if they never give it back?

Shut up, I answered and began plotting. I'd find a way out of this shithole. When I did, I'd make Mother, Father, and the Sidhe sorry they'd crossed me. No matter what Mother said, I was destined to be the Sidhe queen.

And I'd rule with an iron hand. I'd be beautiful and terrible. The Sidhe would cower before me—and do my bidding.

A smile formed, small at first but growing. Mother was right about my childhood being over, but she had no idea quite what that meant.

Once I was free, I'd make certain she rued those words— and a whole lot of other ones. I'd bind animals to me and turn them against her.

Suddenly sleepy, I pushed the dishes to one side, laid my head on folded arms, and shut my eyes. If my jailers wanted me, they could jolly well wake me up.

CHAPTER 5
BLAKE

I walked deeper into the wilds, growing more used to the thin air. Nothing much here. Certainly no vampires. It wasn't a part of the world where they'd established residency. I'm nothing if not thorough, so I kept at it for a full half hour before turning around and retracing my steps. Travis and Jonik were at our appointed meeting spot.

"Find anything?" I kept my voice low.

"Nothing from me," Travis said.

"Only a handful of vampires," Jonik added, "and they were in stasis. From the looks of it, they'd been there for a long while."

I narrowed my eyes. Perhaps it was some sort of punishment or a standard rotation to save on nourishment supplies. While in stasis, vampires didn't feed. Fewer mouths meant less blood was needed to go around.

Speaking of which... "Did you see anything here that might provide food?"

Both men shook their heads. Fascinating. I hadn't, either. If animals lived here, my magic hadn't pinpointed them. More pertinently, if any animals roamed here, they'd have found Abria.

I looked around expecting her to pop into sight at any moment. Five minutes ticked past, and then five more. "We have to look for her," I told the others.

"We expected as much," Jonik said.

I widened my ward to include us all, and we struck out to the north. Soon the dirt track turned into a cobblestone roadway. Buildings came into view. Aha. This was the direction leading to their settlement.

Had Abria walked into a trap?

I closed my teeth over my lower lip but stopped shy of drawing blood. Did I dare risk a bit of a seeking spell to locate her? If I were quick about it, maybe no one would notice. After motioning for the others to stop, I drilled a small hole in my ward and shot a beam of power through it. The whole operation couldn't have taken more than ten seconds.

It gave me what I needed.

Keeping silent, I motioned the others forward. We came to a walled city not unlike some in medieval Europe. The gate was closed. Had Abria scaled the wall? Unlikely. She might have employed power to jump over it, but a stunt like that would have alerted every vampire in a fifty-meter radius.

We followed the wall around until I located exactly what

I expected to find. A small postern gate offered access. Naturally, it was bolted shut, but I made short work of the rusty lock.

We slithered through.

Empty streets suggested everyone had ganged up on Abria.

Fear for her seared me; I beat it back. A cool head would buy me more than flattening everything around us. Scorched earth would be satisfying—after Abria was safe.

Locating a likely alleyway, I hurried along it until we reached the building Abria had holed up in. As I'd suspected, many vampires were inside along with her.

Travis motioned to me. I got the drift. He was saying we were badly outnumbered. But in the time it would take to return to Underhill for reinforcements, Abria could sustain damage.

Perhaps she already had.

A series of ladders were attached to the side of the stone building. Better to use them than to sashay through the only door. Drawing Jarik and Travis close, I whispered. "Ladders to the roof. From that point, we'll join our magic and whisk her out of there."

Travis arched a brow in an unspoken question. I nodded understanding and added, "We'll build a travel spell. Once it's ready, I'll send a separate bit of power to grab her. And then, we're gone."

"What if she fights you?" Jarik whispered back.

Mmph. Good point. "Once we're ready," I told him, "I'll let her know what we're doing."

"We have to be quick," Travis mumbled.

"Aye, the enchantment from our journey spell is a dead giveaway," Jarik cut in.

Irritation singed me. Rather than highlighting all the ways my plan could run aground, I'd have much preferred them focusing on its strengths. Our only other option was to burst into the room, power blazing, and hope for the best. By my count, at least fifty vampires crowded into the chamber where Abria was trapped with still more spilling into hallways and other nooks and crannies.

We could always resort to brute force, if I couldn't extricate her with magic.

"Craft a travel spell. Begin on my count of three." I kept my voice low. "One. Two. Three."

We all pulled power, being as subtle as we could. In less than a minute, our exit route blazed before us, gateway glowing a soft white. I activated my link with Abria and employed telepathy.

"We're here. Do not fight us."

She didn't answer. I assumed she'd heard me, visualized where I'd felt her presence, and corralled power into a net to snag her. Peering through my third eye, I saw her and the enchanted netting as it settled around her.

In a single fluid act, I ignited that part of my spell. Thick glowing lines burst through the rooftop, surrounding us.

"What the hell?" Travis sounded rattled.

"Ley lines," I said.

We'd been quiet before. No more. I turned to the nearest line and bowed. "I am Abria's mate. I was present when she healed you."

The line swayed, glowed brighter, and apparently

released whatever chokehold it had on my summoning spell. Abria popped into view. Hands raised, lightning forking from her fingertips, and mouth twisted into a rictus, she looked like an elemental force of nature.

A horizontal gash ran along one cheekbone. Dried blood decorated her face. She'd kept the vampire horde at bay, but it had cost her.

So far, so good.

Or not.

Jarik and Travis were so unnerved by the ley lines, they'd let go of our escape hatch. "Build that travel spell," I hissed. "Now."

"Aye, Regent." Jarik bowed.

Vampires poured onto the roof. We'd lost the advantages of speed and stealth. I sank into a crouch and shot blasts of power, not trying to kill but to move them into freefall off the roof. If I could get rid of enough of them, we'd have time to get the fuck out of this shithole.

Abria joined me. Back to back, we pushed one vampire after another off the rooftop. To my absolute shock, some spread wings and flew right back in my face. When not in use, their wings are invisible. Neat trick. Or maybe they hide them with a glamour much the way I do when I walk among mortals.

Didn't matter which.

What did was this was beginning to feel like shooting kewpie dolls in an amusement gallery. They went down and bounced back laughing in your face.

"Ready, Regent," Jarik shouted.

A quick glance showed a wavery gateway. Ley lines

slithered into position in front of it, guarding it from vampires. Incredible—and welcome—to have them at our beck and call.

"Go through," I told Abria.

"Ha. Not a chance without you." She took aim, and three vampires tumbled backward off the flat rooftop. So far, none had gotten near enough to mete out any harm.

"Can the lines clear the field?" I asked.

I couldn't see her face, but I'd bet my last pound note she was smiling when she said, "Watch them."

Leaving her position back to back with me, she knelt next to a line and wrapped her hands around it. Her flesh took on a translucent glow as she communicated our needs.

Working as a unit, the lines rose up creating a barrier between us and the vampires. "Leave," I snapped at Travis and Jarik.

They didn't wait for further orders. Between the lines and the sheer number of vampires, they wanted to be gone from this place.

"Now you," I told Abria.

She was back upright. Lacing her fingers with mine, she said, "We do this together."

We walked through, and I said words to close the portal behind us. It telescoped, ballooned out, and guttered like a dying candle but not before depositing a vampire on our side.

He'd somehow defeated the barrier created by the ley lines. How had it happened?

Fangs gleamed in the low light of the journey spell. He advanced toward us, wings pinned tight against his back.

"No one," he said in heavily accented Gaelic, "trespasses on our world without consequence."

Travis and Jarik joined us. Steel glistened in their hands as they drew blades.

Might work. A stake through the heart was one way of dealing with these bastards. But it had to be silver.

"Don't kill him," Abria shouted. "Torture him until he tells us what he knows."

Our whole purpose had been to glean details about the plan to kidnap our daughter. "Any ideas how to accomplish that?" I asked never taking my eyes from the vampire. If he chose, he could blow our travel channel to smithereens, stranding all of us—including him—in the in-between place.

The vampire lunged at Abria, catching the side of her face with long filthy nails. Blood flowed. His tongue extended reflexively, fangs locked into place and growing longer. Blood was everything to him, the elixir of life. Funny analogy to use for a creature that had probably been dead for centuries.

I threw my body between them, snarling.

"She is mine, Sidhe. I made her bleed."

"I think not."

The other Sidhe flanked me. Travis thrust his blade deep into the vampire's chest. When he withdrew it, black, stinking ichor flowed lazily, pooling at the vampire's feet.

"You can't kill me," the vampire sneered. "I'm already dead. Quite convenient, all in all."

How far was Underhill? I couldn't divert my attention to

check. Once we emerged, the magical land would step in and assist us.

Jarik repeated Travis's blade action, hitting the vampire's other side. Next to me, Abria swayed alarmingly. I wrapped an arm around her to steady her. "What's wrong."

"Nothing. Everything. Dizzy." Her eyes closed; she sagged against me. If I wasn't holding her, she'd have sunk to the bottom of the journey channel.

"Told you, Sidhe. She is mine. I marked her. Only I can bring her back." He raised a wrist and nicked it with a fang. Dark blood pooled. "Come close little mage," he purred.

To my horror, Abria jerked upright and tried to wriggle from my grasp.

"No." My tone was sharp; I shackled her with power.

She writhed in my grip, twisted, and bit my shoulder.

What in the goddess's name? I'd heard about vampiric mesmerism but thought it was relegated to mortals. Tightening my hold on her, I said, "Fight this."

"Don't want to." She strained toward the vampire.

Shiny chestnut hair hung midway down his chest. Chocolate eyes were nested beneath strong brows. Something about being turned confers an otherworldly beauty. I always assumed they needed it to attract food sources. A plaid woolen shirt unbuttoned partway; skintight jeans showcased a Chippendales body with broad shoulders and long legs. Black loafers crafted from soft leather cradled his feet.

"Get hold of yourself." I tried again.

Twisting her head, she spat in my face. "Unhand me, or I'll sic the ley lines on you."

"Irrelevant. They can't get into where we are," I informed her.

"What makes you so sure?"

"Let her go, Sidhe," the vampire urged. "She will ache for me all the rest of her days. You've become an anachronism."

"Like hell I have."

Unlike Abria, anger is far from my go-to place, but it swept through me now. My vision hazed red. I shoved Abria into Travis's arms. "Hang on to her, no matter what."

I advanced on the vampire determined to wipe the shit-eating grin off his face, once and for all.

"Give it up, Sidhe. My power is older than yours. If we wished, we could rule the magical world, but we prefer things as they are."

"That's a boldfaced lie," I growled. "Hiding out on a subpar planet with a barely breathable atmosphere isn't anyone's idea of paradise."

"We are not hiding." He managed to sound injured. "It is our home."

Underhill chose that moment to snap into reality around us. We stood in the central hall in front of the council chamber. The vampire's smooth, unruffled countenance developed a few lines. Had he not anticipated this moment? Surely, he hadn't thought we'd drift forever.

Sidhe rushed up from all sides. "Take him," I ordered.

"Where, Regent?" Travis asked.

"Underhill's dungeons. Secure him with metal and magic." I took over hanging onto Abria.

She was screaming imprecations and using all her strength to join the vampire. Kicking, hissing, spitting.

Hanging onto her developed all the joy of dealing with a pissed-off mountain lion. It didn't get better when a dozen Sidhe surrounded the vamp and herded him down a nearby hallway.

Kirwan hurried to my side, sized up the situation, and dropped a golden cage around Abria and me. "Let go," he instructed. I did, and ended up outside the enclosure.

"It will hold her for now," Kirwan explained.

"What's wrong with her?" I asked.

"The creature marked her, injected her with desire for him."

"I figured out that part," I said dryly. "How can we fix it?"

The old mage shook his head. "Not sure. Need to research it. Meanwhile, she must be secured. Perhaps with our healers."

"Nay. I will bring her to our quarters."

"Watch over her," he cautioned. "If she activates her link with animals or the lines, we're all in for a rough ride."

I made shooing motions. "Hurry. Find the antidote."

"Not sure there is one," he mumbled before scurrying away.

I built enchantment and moved her, me, and the cage to our quarters. Once inside, I sealed the door. The woman screeching she hated me and clawing at the enclosure bore scant resemblance to the one I'd pledged my life to.

She pulled at her hair. Her eyes rolled back in her head just before she collapsed in a heap. I crafted power to dismantle the cage, but reeled it in. I'd wait for Kirwan before I did anything.

Reaching deep, I connected with Underhill. *"Help me. Return my love to me unscathed."*

A feral moan suggested Abria was sinking into madness. Was that what happened when a vampire's victim was deprived of their bloodsucking master?

Grateful she'd stopped cursing me, I settled in to wait. It was hard. I felt pressed to do something, anything.

"Doing the wrong thing is worse than doing nothing," I muttered.

She was sobbing now. It tore my heart out not to hold her close and comfort her, but it wasn't me she wanted.

Somehow, beyond wisdom or reason, the vampire had snatched her affection.

As I sat, staring at the cage and my darling, an idea took shape. I'd wait for Kirwan and run it past him, but if he didn't come up with a firm strategy that promised success, we'd implement my plan.

CHAPTER 6
ABRIA

What was wrong with me? After the piece of shit vampire cut my face, I turned into two people, except the normal me was buried six feet under and couldn't make so much as a peep. I didn't get it. Other vamps had drawn blood. Why was this so different?

No. Wait. The other vampire, the ancient, wicked one from the battle almost thirteen years ago, hadn't gotten close enough to touch me. Why would I remember it differently? What in the goddess's name was happening to me? Was I losing my mind—along with everything else?

Breathe, a tiny, distant inner voice directed.

I drew a long shuddery breath and understood I'd given up the practice. Did it mean I was on my way to being dead? The only part left to complete my transformation was drinking from the vampire's wrist. He'd nicked the artery that ran beneath his beautiful, alabaster skin. A reddish-black bubble had formed, beckoning me to suckle.

And I'd wanted to. So badly it shocked me, drove every angstrom of sense from my mind.

Even before that luscious blood bubble, I'd smelled the nectar flowing through his veins. An elixir that would promise me life everlasting...

I already had that, though. I was immortal. And I could manage it as a living, breathing being, not an undead abomination.

I ground my teeth, curled my hands into fists. Shrieks burst from my abraded throat, and I was saying horrid things. Calling Blake names I didn't mean. All because I had to have what the vampire offered.

"Call him back," I yelled knowing there was no coming back from the Sidhe dungeons. Even Sidhe can't escape their clutches. The vampire had no chance at all.

Without him, I'd die.

I shook myself hard. I wasn't thinking straight. I did not need to transition into anything. Immortality was already mine.

Fuck! I'd quit breathing again. Somehow, I ended up a heap on the floor of the cage Blake had chucked me into. Because I was incapable of splitting my attention, I halted the flow of invectives spewing from me and concentrated on breathing. Just breathing.

In. Hold. Out.

In. Hold. Out.

As long as I was breathing, I hadn't been subsumed into the ranks of the undead. At least, I didn't think I had. I knew less than nothing about vampires, an oversight I'd remedy just as soon as I got out from under the current problem.

I kept it up until the next breath happened automatically, like they were supposed to. But I still didn't trust it and added numbers to the mix. I breathed in on one, out on two.

Simple enough.

Meanwhile, Blake had positioned himself in a chair next to my impromptu prison. The look in his eyes drove a spear through my heart. I read despair and desperation in his expression and in every line of his body from the slumped shoulders to his furrowed forehead.

He loved me. Adored me. His lips moved, but I couldn't hear him. Was he talking to me or himself? Did I dare move my attention off my breath long enough to try telepathy?

I reached for my power—and ran into a brick wall.

Bullshit.

No one. Not the yummy vampire with his alluring blood or anyone else separates me from who I am.

Kirwan was back in the room. He and Blake appeared to be in the midst of a heated discussion. Why couldn't I hear them? When had Kirwan shown up? Why was my life happening in snatches? Other than the cadence of my breathing, nothing was unfolding in any sort of logical sequence.

With gargantuan effort, I dragged myself upright by grabbing the bars of my prison. They were imbued with magic that seared my palms. Pain didn't stop me. Neither did the stench of my own flesh burning.

Kirwan pointed at me and made a sigil against evil.

I hissed at him. Power flew from his fingertips, but the edge of my cage deflected it. Blake doubled up a fist. I silently cheered him on, hoping he'd deck Kirwan, but then I pulled myself up short.

I might be breathing, but no part of anything else was remotely like the old me.

Blake dropped his arm to his side and flexed his fingers.

Kirwan sketched something in the air with runes. Blake obliterated a couple, reworking the magical equation. The two of them stared at it and made a few more changes.

Meanwhile, I'd quit breathing again.

Crap.

It was easier this time to fall into my *in, hold, out* routine, but I clearly wasn't out of the woods. Whatever the vampire had imbued with his scratch was still at work wreaking havoc within me.

I tried to reach my magic again.

And failed.

The runic circus was growing. It almost circled my prison.

Not a prison, I corrected myself. Blake had corralled me to keep me from harming myself or spreading whatever was wrong with me to him or any of the Sidhe.

He has a tough job. One I hadn't made any simpler. I vowed to be more sensitive to, well to everything, once I broke free.

Two final runes fell into place. Pain streamed into me from every side. Hot. Cold. Sharp. Prickly. A low keening burst from me. Hell if I didn't sound like a wounded animal.

Animals.

Why hadn't they raced to me, surrounded me, offered love and comfort?

I was in trouble. Couldn't they sense my distress?

Apparently not. I answered my own question.

Fueled by pain, anger streamed through me. Suddenly, the schism that had plagued me since the vamp got his claws into my face shattered. Clarity took its place. In no universe did I want to join the ranks of the undead.

More to the point, I heartily wished destruction would rain down on every single vampiric piece of shit and wipe them out everywhere they had the temerity to rear their icky, undead heads.

The pain hadn't abated. Instead of withering beneath its onslaught, I grabbed onto it, integrated it, fed off the energy it gave me. My jail had developed an opaque aspect. I couldn't see either Blake or Kirwan through its weave.

I felt them though, felt their magic. I'd never realized how different one was from the other. In the past, Sidhe power had been the same, for the most part. I'd never noticed the nuanced aspects—until now.

Oh-oh, I hadn't been paying attention. Had I quit breathing again? Almost fearing to check, I did anyway. Relief spilled through me. Finally, the flow of life-giving air was back on autopilot.

Runes swirled around my enclosure. I could barely make them out, but when they switched direction, I felt the tug of their power. Finally, the siren song of vampiric glory faded. I reached for my magic again, stretched after it with every sinew of my being.

And caught a glimpse. The wall I'd run up against before was still there, but it wasn't as solid. I could see through it.

"Try, Abria," reached a distant corner of my mind. Faint, weak, but Blake's voice clear as anything.

I nodded to let him know I'd heard. Whether he could see me through the whirling vapors was a big unknown, but I respected his skill.

"I am." I thought the words and hoped they'd somehow drill through to him.

I waited through a count of one hundred before I made one more attempt to lasso my erstwhile magic. It had been robust, unbreakable—until now.

I'm not the praying type. For one thing, who would I pray to? Certainly not any of the mortals' gods, nor the Celts who'd jettisoned me. Didn't leave much. But I floated a prayer to the universe, nonetheless.

And then I gave it everything I had. The sensation of hot and cold knives gouging my flesh intensified tenfold. Screams billowed around me. Took a while before I understood they were coming from me. Power caught me up, spun me around, and tossed me this way and that, its flow sweet and familiar.

Power. My power was alive once more. I would never, never take it for granted again.

Screams ceded to jagged laughter and huge sloppy sobs.

Blake and Kirwan argued on. I could finally hear them. Hallelujah.

"She's back, I tell you," Blake shouted.

"Wait. It could be one more vampiric trick," Kirwan cautioned.

"The vampire is buried a hundred meters under." Blake was still shouting.

"You have to believe that. You love her." Kirwan's tone was placating.

"Damn straight I do," Blake thundered, "but it doesn't make me a patsy or a fool."

The bars of my prison rattled like chains as Blake's power fought with Kirwan's.

"I'm all right," I shouted.

Neither mage so much as batted an eyelash my way.

Fine.

I switched to telepathy. *"I'm okay. Truly I am,"* I said.

This time, two sets of eyes swiveled in my direction. Both mages planted their feet, staring dead at me as if they could determine the truth in my statement by visual inspection.

We stood like that as minutes dribbled past. Why didn't Blake pull rank and tell Kirwan to stand down?

Because he's not sure...

His internal struggle twisted his features into a tormented mask. Caught between love, duty, and despair, Blake held his ground. He'd do what was best for me and for his people, not putting one ahead of the other.

In that moment, I developed a whole new level of respect for my mate. A steady core and unshakeable moral compass dictated his actions. He'd do what was best for me, not most convenient. If waiting meant not losing me to evil, he'd have infinite patience.

The vampire still clamored for ascendency, but it was

simple to shove him aside. How to rid myself of him completely?

Good question.

I ran my fingertips down my abraded cheek. The wounds were still there. Focusing my newly resurrected magic, I sent healing water mixed with earth to repair my abrasions. They shrank beneath my fingertips until only smooth skin remained. Along with them, the last vestiges of my would-be master vanished.

Blake and Kirwan must have come to an agreement.

The walls around me clattered to the floor. The runes still skipped in a circle, but their frantic quality had lessened.

I started toward Blake. He held out a hand; my steps faltered. Why couldn't he believe in me? I wouldn't put him at risk.

Roll the clock back an hour or so, and I sure as hell would have, a sour inner voice reminded me.

The familiar feel of his magic surrounded me, poking and prodding. Kirwan added to the mix, none too gently. I remained still beneath their examination, determined to not make them regret freeing me.

The men exchanged glances. Kirwan nodded. Blake opened his arms; I stepped into them. When he embraced me, I sagged against him and clung to his muscled frame before my knees gave out.

A Sidhe I didn't recognize raced into the room—my living room—and skidded to a halt, shouting, "Regent. The vampire is dead."

"Tell me something I don't know," Blake growled.

The Sidhe shook his head and fell to one knee, a fist clapped to his breastbone. "No, Regent. Truly dead, as in a pile of bones. It happened so fast, it caught us by surprise. One minute he was standing in his cell shaking the bars, the next, his fingers turned to naught but bone, and then he was all bones in an untidy pile scattered in the dirt."

I untangled a hand from behind Blake's back and stroked my healed cheek. Had I unleashed mayhem on him when I'd driven him from my body?

"Appreciate you letting me know," Blake was saying. "Make certain you salt and burn what's left to ensure he can never return."

"Aye, Regent." The Sidhe hustled from the room.

Blake settled his hands on my shoulders. His dark gaze drilled into me. "Good to have you back," he said gruffly.

"You gave us quite a fright." Kirwan patted my arm.

The old mage isn't given to flights of hyperbole. For him to go that far meant he'd figured I was lost to darkness.

"I gave me a fright," I told him. "It was like I was two people, but when I realized I'd quit breathing, I panicked."

A sound between a moan and a grunt escaped Blake. "Damn it. I had no idea it was that close."

His words sent a torrent of ice chips cascading down my spine.

"Do you know why the vampire ended up a heap of bones?" I glanced from Blake to Kirwan and back again before adding, "Surely, they lose the occasional victim. If it was that simple to end them, they'd have died out long since."

Kirwan nodded knowingly. "It was as I told you." He sent a

pointed look winging Blake's way. "He was linked to the world where you found him in such a way he couldn't leave. Unless he staked a claim to another being living in the place he ended up."

Breath rattled from Kirwan. "One of the main reasons vampires haven't proliferated more widely is they cannot travel far from the place they were turned. No one knows precisely what that distance is, and I've always suspected it varies depending on how old and powerful the vampire was, but they require a blood link to whichever new spot they choose to relocate."

I crinkled my forehead, thinking. "What about the creature we fought almost thirteen years ago. He was a vampire, and he didn't seem to have any trouble transiting worlds."

"He was also a mage." Blake's voice was soft. "He began as a mage and added vampiric powers to the mix."

"It made him one of a kind," Kirwan growled, "since not many of us would choose the undead life. Not when we're already immortal."

I touched my cheek. "When I healed the wounds he'd inflicted, I already had my power back, and—"

"You lost your magic?" Blake asked incredulously.

I nodded. "Yeah. It was gone."

"Ha." Blake nudged Kirwan. "You worried about her laying waste to Underhill for nothing."

"Perhaps so. Better safe than sorry, though."

"I agree," I piped up. "Completely."

"We still don't know anything about their plot to kidnap Tiana," Blake murmured. "I'd planned to interrogate the vampire."

"Too late now," Kirwan tossed out. "Not that he'd have told you anything. His kind can be remarkably close-mouthed. They're impervious to pain. It makes torture a waste of time."

Interesting. The crash course I'd wanted in Vampire 101 was happening all around me.

"We'll have to figure something else out," I said, suddenly aware how wiped out I was. The adrenaline must be fading. I swayed from foot to foot determined not to pitch facedown on the richly embroidered rug.

"I should go," Kirwan said.

Blake stuck out a hand. The other mage clasped it. "Thanks, mate."

"You'd have done the same for me." Turning, Kirwan plodded out of our suite of rooms.

The snick of the door shutting behind him was my signal to fall into the nearest chair. "What did he mean by that?" I asked. "Did Kirwan have a mate?"

Blake barked a few words. Platters laden with fresh bread, fruit, cheese, and a quiche-looking item floated past and plonked on a nearby table. He filled a plate, handed it to me, and got one for himself.

When he hooked a chair with a booted foot, it ended up across from me. He didn't exactly do a swan dive into it, but damned close. He shut his eyes; a labored breath whooshed from him.

"That bad?" I tried for a bantering note and failed miserably.

"Aye, and worse, but it's over. We came out on top. For

now." He hesitated. "You asked about Kirwan. He was mated long ago."

I stopped chewing. First I'd heard anything about his history. "And?" I twirled one hand in a come-along gesture."

"We lost her during the war with the Dark Fae."

I did a few quick mental calculations. "The one that happened in the 1500s?"

"Close enough."

"What do you mean by lost? Wasn't she immortal?"

Blake nodded. "She's in the *Dreaming*, but something happened to her mind. The Dark Fae captured her. By the time Kirwan and I effected a rescue, she'd gone mad." He closed his teeth over his lower lip hard enough to leave indentations. "We tried everything. Nothing made a dent. Some of our efforts made things worse. Finally, we left her to her ravings and wanderings. At least naught can harm her further.

"Kirwan visits every month. He's stoic, but he's never given up hope Emilie will recover."

I finally understood why some days were off limits for Tiana's lessons.

A tankard of mead sat next to me. I hadn't noticed its arrival, but I picked it up and drained it. A pleasant haze put distance between me and nearly losing myself to vampiric mesmerism.

I ate methodically, more to ensure my power recovered fully than anything else. The clink of silver on china told me my plate was empty. When I looked up, Blake's gaze snared me. His eyes betrayed more than he probably wanted me to see.

He hadn't been joking when he'd alluded to how close I'd come to annihilation.

"Are you sorry you married me?" I blurted, needing to know.

"Abria. Why even ask such a question?" On his feet in a trice, he dragged me upright and clasped me against him.

"It was simpler when all you had to worry yourself with was the Sidhe."

Rather than answer, he crushed his mouth over mine. Whenever we touched, it was just him and me. Today was no exception. Fear and exhaustion ceded to sweet, hot lust setting my nerve endings on fire.

After wrapping my arms tightly around Blake, I opened my mouth to the magic of his tongue and stopped thinking entirely.

CHAPTER 7
BLAKE

Once again, Abria had rescued herself. She'd done it before when captured deep in Satan's realm, and again when she'd been subsumed by the ley lines. This time, I'd have trusted her innate ability more were it not for Kirwan's reticence. Maybe he'd been tainted by centuries of failure to bring his own love back from where she wandered.

Every healer the Sidhe ever spawned had worked tirelessly on Emilie—to no avail. To his credit, Kirwan hadn't become bitter. Resigned, but he didn't blame anyone for her plight. War carried risks. This time round, she'd paid the price. No matter how many enchantments had been cast her way, Emilie remained oblivious to much of anything.

At least she wasn't suffering. If aught remained of her old life, my bet was she didn't recall much.

My mind had taken off on a tangent, a diversion to allow breathing space. When the vampire drew blood, I'd been certain Abria couldn't escape his pull. I'd never known anyone to stop between that step and the next: drinking blood to complete the ritual.

Without dying.

A few hardy souls were so disgusted by the specter of an eternal undead life, they turned away from the flow of sustaining ichor. Turned away, and faded from whatever world anchored them.

I'd been quick to remove the vampire and surround Abria with what I hoped was an unbreakable barrier. If she'd called on the ley lines, though, nothing I built could have withstood their onslaught.

Maybe.

For all I knew Abria had summoned them, and they'd wisely looked the other way. She was daughter to the lines, not their master. And she'd said magic deserted her when she was in thrall to the vampire.

So far, the lines had been circumspect where Tiana was concerned. They'd neatly skirted sharing power with her. Quite the relief since she lacked sufficient maturity to be trusted with any more magic than she already commanded.

I finished eating, barely remembering what crossed my lips. We'd talked about Kirwan's lost mate, but nothing else of substance. I wanted Abria to recover. Quizzing her about her experience was counterproductive. When she asked if I was sorry I'd married her, I kicked myself for not doing a better job glossing over the angst that still had me in its grip.

Raw and unfettered, it was as clear a message as I was likely to get that I had to pay better attention.

To everything.

Trapped between my fears for Abria and equally potent fears she'd run amok and bite every Sidhe in her path, I'd hesitated when I should have acted. The time to be vigilant was before the vampire struck.

Instead, I'd been caught up in damage control. My lightning-quick decisions had panned out, but far better to have been three steps ahead rather than two behind.

Abria's question was a knife twisting in my guts. I sprang to my feet and crushed her against me, saying with my body what I couldn't with my tongue. We were tired and filthy, still stinking of the field and vampire taint.

None of it mattered.

I pressed my tongue inside her mouth. She bit the tip and then sparred with it. With our mouths glued together, I ripped the fabric of her top down the back and tossed the pieces aside. Nails gouged my neck, dug into my shoulders, and yanked at my leather jerkin. A shrug and a shot of magic removed it along with the woolen shirt beneath.

Bare breasts smashed into my naked flesh. My heart pounded; my throat was dry. Breath came fast as lust dug its claws into me. She ripped her mouth from mine and panted, "The worst part was I quit breathing. And I didn't even notice."

This time when I kissed her, I was gentle, a promise of what we'd always meant to one another and always would. My words were lost in her sea of fiery hair, but she'd hear them anyway. "You're strong, leannan. No matter how bad things are, how desperate, you never, never stop trying.

"I love you for it."

She nuzzled my neck. Her nipples had turned to peaks where they rubbed against me. "I love you too, but a wiser man would have fed me to the cassowaries long since."

"Haven't met one of them in a long while. Here." Reaching between us, I unfastened her trousers and then realized she still wore boots. I knelt, stringing kisses down her flesh as I moved lower and unlaced her footwear by feel. She slithered out of her boots by balancing with a hand on my shoulder.

With nothing to impede their downward progress, her pants glided down her long legs. She stepped out of them. The musk of her hit me with all the subtlety of a frost giant on a rampage. I covered her sex with my mouth, sucking greedily, and slipped two fingers inside her body.

She made a sound between a lioness on the prowl and a moan as she bucked against my touch. All too soon, she convulsed against me, shuddering with delight as one climax followed another. My cock strained against the fabric of my pants, but I was too busy to pay it any heed. I'd suck and swirl until she was a puddle of satiated faery dust.

Moans turned to shrieks as she writhed between my fingers and mouth. I wasn't gentle. Now wasn't a time for gentle. It was a time to reclaim what was ours—what had nearly been snatched away.

Her legs trembled, and then she slid from my grasp, joining me on the floor where she unlaced my britches and covered my aching hardness with her mouth. Sensation cascaded through me, lighting every nerve ending. Brilliant light surrounded us, courtesy of the lines. I drank it in, and it intensified everything.

No woman has ever had this effect on me where each time we make love we're as hungry as if we were brand new together. The heat from her mouth and scratches from her teeth were alluring, magical, but what I wanted was to bury myself in the wonder of her body.

I lifted her head from my shaft, rolled onto my back, and wriggled around until she straddled me with all her slick heat. I brushed hair back from her face, framing it with my hands so I could look at her, lose myself in the depths of her emerald eyes when release took me.

I called magic to make this last. I wanted to plunge in and out of her forever as ecstasy spilled through me. Her gorgeous body, skin blotchy with passion, rose and fell above me as she withdrew and sank onto me. Muscles gripped and relaxed, gripped and relaxed.

My balls had passed the point of pain long since, but still I held off. I longed for these moments to last forever, as if I could imprint her and me and our love into every cell of both our bodies.

Finally, long, slow, lazy gouts of semen exploded. No magic in the world could have held them back at that point. She crested with me and then collapsed across my body, heaving and panting and crying.

I cradled her, stroked her hair, murmured in Gaelic until she fell asleep, and then I added calming spells to ensure she didn't waken as I extricated myself from her body. Rising, I carried her to our bed and laid her tenderly on soft furs. We could wash once she woke. For now, I'd keep watch over her, surround her with my arms and wings, and ensure nothing disturbed her rest.

I admit to dozing off a time or two, but never for long. The gentle rise and fall of her breasts reassured me the vampire's grip was truly broken. It had to be. He was naught but bones, and ones that had been salted and burned by now.

We weren't any closer to knowledge about their plans to shanghai our daughter. Judging from our visit to their borderworld and my interactions with the one who'd jumped into our return travel spell, no torture within my repertoire could wrest secrets from that bunch.

Perhaps Jonik and Travis were mistaken. Or not so much mistaken as lacking relevant details. The plot to nab Tiana might include many dark mages. Vampires could be a small portion of the problem.

When I shut my eyes, the lids could have been lined with ground glass. Scratchy and hot, they reminded me how long since I'd truly rested.

Get over it, I growled silently. There'd be no rest until we cut the knees out from under whoever was intent on kidnapping Tiana, stripping her power, and ensuring she never got anywhere close to the Sidhe throne.

Breath burbled from me. My daughter might never ascend to anything if she didn't mend her ways. I'd been intent on encouraging her independence to foster leadership qualities.

My pampering had backfired spectacularly.

Rather than growing into levelheaded wisdom, she'd become spoiled, self-indulgent, and lazy, a child who didn't take no for an answer. When she was five, I'd thought it adorable when she spread her tiny wings, puffed out her lower lip, and wheedled her way through things. Abria tried to instill discipline, but I went behind her back and made excuses for Tiana's mishaps. Neither did I insist she apologize when clearly in the wrong.

Sidhe who knew her well didn't care for her but offered her leeway for two reasons: she was the first child born in Underhill in over a century, and she was mine.

Since Oberon and Titania had deserted the Sidhe long ago, we've self-governed via our council structure. The only reason I thought Tiana would be a Sidhe queen was because Arianrhod proclaimed it. Or perhaps it had been Ceridwen. Regardless, the Celts were in agreement.

Who was I to dissent?

The council would have to vote Tiana into office. The way things were going, it would never happen. Breanne viewed her as a spoiled brat. Kirwan's patience had worn thin.

Hopefully, she wasn't wreaking havoc in Caer Sidi. Arianrhod hadn't shown up to dump her on our doorstep. Surely, if Tiana had been in her usual high dudgeon, the goddess would have dropkicked her into our laps immediately.

Abria mumbled in her sleep and pushed closer. I kissed her forehead.

"We should get up." Her words were slurred.

"Another hour or two won't make any difference."

"You never know." Abria kissed the hollow of my collarbone before rolling off the edge of the bed and to her feet.

The sound of running water forced me upright, and I joined her under a scalding shower.

"What should we do next?" she asked.

"You've thought about it," I countered. "What do you want to do?"

For once, she didn't turn the shower into a water fight. After she'd closed the taps and covered herself with a thick, white towel, she said, "We have a twofold problem. We need to determine who's after Tiana, but we also need to know why she's such an attractive target."

"Because she's slated to rule the Sidhe."

Abria hung her towel on a hook and shot me a you-know-better look. I finished rinsing soap out of my hair, toweled off, and joined her in the bedroom. She was already dressed in a long black suede skirt and green linen shirt. Boots graced her feet, but they were dressy, not the stout lace-up ones I'd removed.

"I've been thinking about that," she said.

"About what?" I dragged brown linen trousers up my legs and rustled in an armoire for a cream-colored shirt with long full sleeves.

"Our spawn." Abria curled her mouth into a moue. "She may never get anywhere close to the Sidhe crown no matter what Arianrhod prophesied."

Interesting—and eerie—how closely our thoughts on the matter aligned, but I didn't say anything.

"And?" I arched a brow.

"If she lacks the, erm, temperament to assume a position of power in Underhill, why is she so sought after?"

"Probably no one knows what a brat she is." I winced. Characterizing Tiana with her true colors hurt, but I was determined not to repeat my earlier errors. The ones where

I'd turned a blind eye to her failings, hoping she'd grow out of the worst ones. Instead, they'd become worse, more glaring, as she neared maturity.

"She's only twelve." Abria's voice was soft, and she'd obviously been inside my head. "Granted, she doesn't mind well, but she could be worse."

"Or better. I'm grateful Arianrhod hasn't blasted through a portal, holding our daughter by the scruff of her neck."

"It could still happen," Abria reminded me.

I draped an arm around her shoulders, drawing her close. "I want to return to the vampires' world."

"Why?"

"Haven't given up on extricating something useful."

"I think it's a dead end. And I could barely breathe there."

"Precisely why it's a perfect environment for them. They don't have to breathe."

She shuddered. "Don't remind me."

"You don't have to come with me—" I began.

Waving me to silence, she said, "Satan's realm might bear better fruit."

"You're not going alone."

Oops. I'd come off pretty heavy-handed. The set to her shoulders and a mulish expression meant I'd overstepped my husbandly role.

"Of course not," she agreed sweetly after a measured pause. "I'll rustle up Becca and a handful of unicorns."

"Um, don't you think one of us should remain here? In case Arianrhod tires of her auntie role."

"Feel free to stay." Abria placed her hands on her hips and looked across at me.

I'd been paying such close attention to her, the rest of the world fell away. When I felt someone grip my shoulder, I nearly leapt out of my skin. I hadn't seen a portal, hadn't sensed Celtic magic. Once I refocused, Arianrhod and Ceridwen stood in front of a small impromptu altar I'd built.

Having gotten my attention, the goddesses turned their backs to us. Power crackled around them as they conversed.

I'm not used to being a parent, so it took a while to sink in that Tiana wasn't with them.

Abria ducked from beneath my arm and strode to the goddesses. "Welcome to Underhill," she said. "Who is watching Tiana?"

"No one," Arianrhod snapped off the words.

"Child hadn't even been there a handful of hours before she ran off," Ceridwen chucked into the mix. Half a meter taller than me and broad, she wore hunting leathers crafted from soft, pale doeskin with boots laced to knee level. Her eyes were dark, her forehead high. Black hair frosted with silver hung to her waist in multiple braids.

"But Caer Sidi is bulletproof," I protested. Fear for my daughter thickened my throat and made me want to haul off and slug Arianrhod. Why in the hell hadn't she been watching Tiana, as in eyes on her at all times?

"Is Roya missing too?" Abria asked.

I should have floated that question. Tension tightened my muscles to bricks as I awaited a reply.

"Aye. She's gone as well. Someone drilled right through

my layers of protective spells," Arianrhod shot back. "Hard to believe Tiana did it."

"We'll get them back." Ceridwen's words were far from reassuring.

"Only reason we stopped here first was to check if the two of them ended up back in Underhill." Arianrhod cast a hopeful look my way.

"You know damn good and well they aren't here," I shouted and dug my nails into fisted hands. I had to get control of myself. My current scorched universe mode wouldn't do anyone any good.

"At least Roya is with her," Abria murmured.

"Does your changeling hold sufficient power to leave Caer Sidi?" Arianrhod asked pointblank.

"Nay."

"Told you." Ceridwen came close to being smug. "You did a piss-poor job."

"The hell I did," Arianrhod growled.

It was a cryptic exchange, but I didn't have the energy to question what the fuck they were talking about. "We must return to Caer Sidi," I said and summoned power preparatory to leaving.

"Why?" Arianrhod arched a fair brow. "You won't be able to track anything from behind my gates."

"Fine," I retorted. "How about from the front side then?"

"Do you think we didn't already try?" Arianrhod didn't sound the least bit conciliatory. Too late I recalled what a bad idea it was to question the Celts.

About anything.

"We hold her blood." Abria's voice was soft, gentle.

Ceridwen snapped her fingers. Her kettle clattered to the floor next to her, already bubbling. "Excellent idea." She rubbed her hands together, knuckles bony and rings clanking against each other. "One of you get over here and add a few drops to the mix. I'll solve this riddle straight away."

I tripped over my feet in my haste to reach the kettle's rim. Heat from the contents made my eyes water. Abria had already bitten a hole in her finger. Crimson droplets welled and dropped into the kettle. I withdrew the dirk I always carry and added mine for good measure.

Ceridwen withdrew a rod from her black robe, stirred three times clockwise and then three times the other way. A reddish mist rose from the cauldron. I bent close, intent on gleaning whatever showed itself.

Ceridwen raised her upper lip and hissed at me.

Not wanting to interfere with her concentration, I backed off and stood next to Abria. She reached for my hand, and I laced my fingers with hers.

The goddess passed both hands over the top of the kettle, creating runes with her fingers. The kettle hummed and then moaned. Runes formed on its surface, broke up, and were replaced by others.

I read them easily, but they made no sense.

Ceridwen apparently didn't care for the kettle's message because she repeated her actions, but the resultant runes were the same.

Arianrhod stood shoulder to shoulder with her fellow goddess. "Powerful magic cloaks the truth," she muttered.

"What do you mean?" I asked. My tolerance for ambiguity had hit ground zero.

Ceridwen passed a palm over the contents of her kettle. The surface quieted, and she turned toward us. "The kettle has no idea where Roya and Tiana are."

"Yes, but does that mean they're simply too far away to sense?" Abria asked in a surprisingly steady voice.

Ceridwen pressed her lips into a thin line. "No matter where they are, the kettle should be able to find at least Tiana. Blood links are unbreakable."

"Then, why can't it?" I wanted to pound a fist into the nearest wall. So what if the Celts resented being questioned. I wasn't in the mood to take whatever they chose to dole out and be satisfied.

"Because someone with power that supersedes ours is hiding her from us." Arianrhod's tone suggested she was dealing with a mental defective.

A squawk announced Hedrek's arrival. He'd barely touched down before he bowed before Arianrhod. "I did as instructed my lady, but I ran up against one dead end after another. There's not a sufficient trail to track a field mouse, let alone two female mages."

Having delivered his news, he fluttered to Abria's shoulders.

I'd called him back earlier to do some digging in the local vampire seethe, but apparently, Arianrhod's connection with the owl superseded mine.

"I'll alert the Sidhe," I said. "We'll split up. If we have to search every borderworld, we'll locate her."

"Bad idea," Arianrhod gritted.

Abria turned her hands palms up. "If you have a more productive one, let's hear it."

"Show some respect, child."

Abria let go of me and stomped to where the goddesses stood next to the now quiescent kettle. "My child is missing. She may not be particularly likeable, but still she's only a child. I will send word amongst the animals. If she's anywhere they live, they will find her."

"Perhaps." Ceridwen drew out the word.

Abria angled her head to one side. "No perhaps about it."

Arianrhod huffed out a breath. "I stripped her power, assuming it would make her less of a supervision problem. Apparently, I missed some because she managed to give us the slip."

"You what?" I bellowed beyond caring about showing respect for the two goddesses. At least their earlier exchange about a piss-poor job made sense now.

"Did you think to return it?" Abria choked out the words.

Arianrhod clapped her across the back. "Decent idea, child."

A ball glowing with every shade of the rainbow flew from her long-fingered hands. "Do not try to follow it," the goddess cautioned. "Or it might not make it back to Tiana."

Abria's usually ruddy complexion was pale. She dragged power around her.

"Where are you going?" I asked.

"To send word up and down all realms. Tiana is a pain in the rump, but the birds and animals revere her just like they do me. My first stop will be the wolf den, and I'll move on from there."

"Don't forget the unicorns," Ceridwen called after her disappearing form.

"I won't," floated to me just before my wife disappeared taking the owl with her.

The manners that had deserted me made a cameo appearance. "You can stay as long as you'd like," I said gruffly. "I'm calling an emergency council session. All Sidhe both in Underhill and the *Dreaming* will hunt for Tiana."

"For how long?" Arianrhod inquired.

"Until she's found."

I strode from my quarters. Reading between the goddess's words didn't require any magic at all. She was certain Tiana—and Roya—were gone forever. I refused to go there. Not now, and not ever.

It might take a while for Tiana's power to reunite with her, but once it did, she'd find her way back to us. Finally, her high-handed ways would work in her favor. As would her fearlessness.

Power shot from me in all directions as I called my people to my side. They might not love me, but they respected me. And they'd turn over every rock between here and the farthest borderworld hunting for Tiana.

I was certain of it. We're Sidhe, and we take care of our own.

CHAPTER 8
TIANA

When I opened my eyes I was in the same small chamber where I'd eaten and changed out of my wet clothes. No surprises there. Moving prisoners around is a pain in the butt. When you cut to the chase, it's precisely what I was: a prisoner. If I hadn't been so trashed from being unceremoniously ripped from my one true home—

Not my home anymore, a small voice reminded me.

If this was representative of how my parents—who were supposed to love me—acted when the least little bit of trouble reared its head, I'd have to make other arrangements.

But first, I had to find a way out of Caer Sidi.

It had to be possible. If I played along for a while, everyone would drop their guard. When that happened, I'd pounce and be gone so quick and so far madam queen Arianrhod bitch wouldn't know what hit her.

Ha! I could just see her groveling as she tried to explain losing me to my parents. They might not give a crap about me, but, like any other possession, they'd be furious I'd gone missing.

Two birds with one stone. Paybacks for everyone while I did what I did when I wanted, bonded to as many animals as I chose, and generally got on living my life. A stab of magic sent waves of agony rolling through me. I grunted but didn't cry out.

Proud of myself for holding it together despite residual waves of hot, prickly pain jabbing my most vulnerable spots, I let out a tentative breath. Too little and far too late, I tried to construct warding and drape it around myself. My lack of magic put an end to that little project.

Roya sat cross-legged on the ground in a corner watching me. Damn it. I'd forgotten about her. She'd been so still, I'd assumed I was by myself.

If I was planning to go it alone, I'd need to be far more vigilant.

She arched a red brow. "Are we quite done feeling sorry for ourselves?"

I straightened my back, sitting tall in my chair. "You will not speak thusly to us."

Roya dissolved into hoots of laughter. Not sure what I'd expected, but being laughed at rankled. Before I could toss out another command, this one addressing her inappropriate outburst, she gasped out, "Us? So now you're using the imperial we? Hell, your father never even employs it."

I sputtered, at a loss for what to say to shut her up. I did *not* see us as equals, but how to pound that point home?

"This is one of the reasons you're here." Roya softened her tone.

"What might that be?" I ground out.

The changeling Sidhe flowed to her feet, amazingly graceful in our dingy surroundings. "You're stubborn and headstrong with little to no regard for anyone else."

"I am not." I crossed my arms over my unfortunately mostly still-flat chest.

"Uh-huh." Roya reached the table, dragged out the other chair with her foot, and plopped into it. After patting the teakettle with a wrist, she hooked the stump of her hand into the bale and poured herself a cup. "Want one?" she asked.

Disinclined to take anything from her, I shook my head.

"Have it your way." She released the kettle; it clonked onto the wooden tabletop.

"Why didn't you fix your hands?" I blurted. It was none of my affair, but polite wasn't a word in my vocabulary. Particularly not where underlings were concerned.

"A very good question," she agreed. Holding the mug between her stumps, she took a sip. The scents of mint, cinnamon, and rosemary wafted across to me and made me wish I hadn't been so hasty about declining my own cup of the brew.

When she set the tea down, she waggled a wrist my way and said, "I chose to keep things this way as a reminder."

"Of what?" I rolled my eyes. What could be important enough to remain crippled for life?

"Your father stole me from my human family when I was naught but a babe and too young to hold many memories. I was raised in Underhill until I was a bit older than you. At first, it was difficult, since magic didn't come easily to me. I had to learn everything from scratch, and some tasks still proved too difficult."

I blew out a breath. "Why are you telling me this? It's boring."

The corners of her mouth twitched into a smile. "Your parents were right about you. You're rude and entitled. The reason I'm telling you is you asked why I hadn't employed magic to regrow my hands—or have the Sidhe healers do the same. If you don't want to know, I can stop anytime."

"Go ahead. We've nothing else to do."

A small furrow formed between her brows. I figured she was about to say something else derogatory about me. Instead, she nodded and said, "Very well. Another changeling was growing up in Underhill alongside me. We grew close, probably because we were kind of odd men out.

"When we were fifteen, your father set us to guard one of the portals into Underhill. It was a very important one. Had mortals discovered it, many would have died trying to cross the veil into Faery.

"To make things simpler, your father spun magic to make my family believe I was one of their natural-born children. He did the same for Holder, the other changeling."

My ears had perked up. Contrary to my assertion, her tale was intriguing. "Go on," I urged.

"As luck would have it"—Roya's lips curved into a bittersweet expression—"the homes we went to were rival clans. I overheard my foster father and his brothers plotting against Holder's clan. They planned to slaughter them."

She pressed her lips together. "I couldn't stand by and do nothing. By now, Holder and I had become lovers. We had a trysting spot near the edge of an old graveyard. The next time we met, I told him about the plot against his kinsmen. When we left one another's arms that dawn, I knew I'd never see him again. Not alive, anyway."

A tear formed in the corner of one eye and dripped down her pale cheek. Why was she still so upset? This had happened hundreds of years ago.

"Because Holder was my one true love," she said softly.

My eyes widened. I'd warded my thoughts, yet she'd drilled through my protections handily. Oh yeah. I only thought I'd warded them. The no-magic crap was getting old fast.

"The very next night," she went on, "Holder and his clan arrived for supper. My family had invited them under the guise of forming a truce. Holder's relatives had knives and swords hidden beneath their cloaks. A bloodbath ensued. I lost track of Holder.

"At the end, nearly everyone was dead—except my foster father. He'd figured out I was the guilty party who'd blown the whistle on his plans and chased me through the castle. I was hanging from an upper story window when he chopped off my hands."

My mouth gaped open. "That's horrid. Why didn't you raise power against him?"

"'Tis forbidden."

Her words hit me in the solar plexus. And highlighted the differences between her and me. She played fair. And I, well, I took care of number one first." A shiver trickled down my spine.

"Blake found me," she went on, "and brought me to the *Dreaming*. He offered to fix my hands. I declined. I'd made mistakes, big ones. Far better for Holder and his clan to have not shown up citing some last-minute excuse."

Roya shook her head. "I'd been so certain only a couple of mortals would die."

"What happened to Holder?"

"Your father searched for him and found his body, but all magic had departed from it."

I sketched the sigil against evil and mumbled, "Someone figured out what he was and forced the separation."

"Not necessarily," she corrected me. "I believe he was so distraught about his part in the disaster, he broke the bonds and let his sprit fly free." She drained the remainder of her cold tea.

"After my body healed, I remained in the *Dreaming*. I no longer wished to walk among mortals. Neither did I want to be an object of pity in Underhill where everyone else is perfect."

"Why'd you leave?"

"Your father needed me. I owe him a lot. How could I refuse? Besides, I was useful. I saved your mother's life when she was tossed into Underhill by the Cait long before Faery learned to accept her."

Interesting. I'd never heard anything about that before.

"The reason your parents asked if I could accompany you," she went on, "is because once, long ago, I wasn't unlike you. I thought nothing was beyond my control.

These"—she held up her stumps once again—"remind me to remain humble, thoughtful. If I'd had them repaired, I might have forgotten valuable lessons. Not right away, but we live a long time."

Suddenly, I felt small—and painfully young. I looked away and hoped she wasn't mucking through my mind since I couldn't hide anything from her.

"If you're done eating," she said and got to her feet, "we could visit the suite of rooms waiting for us."

Suite, eh? Maybe someone recognized how important I am.

My memory jogged. "Where's the owl?"

"He had to leave."

"Okay, but why?"

Roya shrugged. "Not sure. Blake reached out telepathically; Arianrhod agreed to release Hedrek."

Great. Just great. If Father could talk with the owl, it meant he could talk with me, but he'd chosen not to.

"He can't," Roya pointed out. "You have no magic."

"Stop that." I pounded a fist on the table.

"Which thing?" Her expression was unreadable. "Reminding you of your impoverished condition, or culling thoughts from your mind."

"Both," I ground out.

"Fair enough, but we'll get on better if we're honest with one another."

I opened my mouth to tell her I could care less about getting along with her, that I'd be shut of her soon enough, but thought better of open defiance. She'd drilled a chink in my armor, but it was mending quickly.

I splayed my hands on the table purposefully, to remind her some of us had hands. It was mean and spiteful, but I wasn't in a conciliatory mood. With a slight bow of my head, I said, "Lead out."

The door opened without her touching it; I followed her into the corridor I remembered. Low and curved, it had sconces spaced at intervals with torches to light our way.

Once again, I tried to build a mental map of Caer Sidi, but there were so many twists and turns, I felt certain we'd come in a circle. Perhaps we had, or Roya had taken a circuitous route to confuse me.

I rubbed a temple. My mind wasn't as sharp as usual. Probably had something to do with my magic being gone.

"Here we are," Roya said cheerfully and pushed a door that looked just like the other hundred or so we'd passed open with a booted foot. Rather than standing aside for me to enter first, she plowed ahead.

I followed and took in my home away from home. The main room was medium sized with a blue couch against one wall. Two matching soft chairs sat across from it. In the corner was an oak desk with a pile of papers stacked on top. Soft rugs in many colors covered a wooden floor.

Roya had crossed the room and opened a door. "Here is our sleeping chamber," she explained. "That other door leads into the bathroom."

Truth sank in. "I demand my own room."

Another enigmatic smile formed on her mouth. "Demand away, sweetie. This is what we have."

I stamped my foot. "You must treat me with respect. I will be queen of the Sidhe."

Roya rounded on me, dark eyes snapping. "Respect must be earned. So far, you've done precious little to convince me you deserve anything. Not my respect, and certainly not any sort of royal title."

With a swoosh of her long skirt, she strode through the still-open door into the hall slamming it behind her.

I was certain it was locked, but I tested it just the same. Not just locked, but sealed with magic. The magicless of the world—ergo me—would never get out.

I paced from one end of the windowless room to the other. Then I sat on the couch, but not for long. When I made it to the desk, I paged through the stack of papers, realized it was my homework, and groaned.

"Fuck this." I slammed my fist into the wall, yelped, and cradled it against my body. To my horror, tears welled. I dug my fists into my eyes to stop them, but they flowed anyway. I staggered into the bathroom, not even seeing it, and tossed cold water on my face.

It helped. At least I got control of myself.

Acting like a prima donna was dumb. All it did was reinforce what they all thought of me. No one would return my magic unless I proved myself. I'd have to pretend to be compliant. Toward that end, after cupping my hands and slurping water, I walked to the desk, settled into the chair, and started on my homework.

Time ticked past. I had no idea how much, but I was deep into a mathematics problem. Interestingly, I didn't hate math as much as I'd thought. It was kind of intriguing when Kirwan wasn't breathing down my neck, tapping his foot, and scowling.

The door snicked open behind me. I didn't bother to turn around.

Roya had come to check on me; I recognized her magic—or thought I did. It takes magic to sense it in others. Good opportunity to unfurl my plan to be a model resident of Caer Sidi. "Just doing homework," I called cheerily.

I never heard footsteps crossing the room. Never sensed anything until something heavy dropped over my head. At first, I figured it was a joke.

"Hey, stop that." My voice was muffled beneath thick woolen folds that had an odd smell to them. Unpleasant and sour.

Someone picked me up and wound something that felt like cord or rope around the blanket. It was tough to breathe. "Let me go!" I shouted. I tried my mind voice, remembered my magic was gone, and yelled for Arianrhod and Roya.

"Behave," a man's accented voice gritted.

"We can do this the easy way or the hard way," another masculine voice informed me, still speaking softly.

"Do what?" I writhed against the blanket and bonds.

"No one likes mouthy children," the first voice said tartly.

"Not a child—" I began.

"Shut her up," the second voice ordered.

The sour stench intensified until I gagged. Puke erupted from me, coating the blanket and my clothes with undigested lunch.

Ewww and ick! I've never enjoyed being dirty, and this

was beyond disgusting. I squirmed, brushed my fingers through vomit to get it off me, and puked some more.

Everything grew fuzzy. My captors said something about "getting the other one." Made no sense. I was the only person here.

Unfamiliar power reeking of sulfur and ozone surrounded me. I tried hard to cling to consciousness, but it eluded me. With the last of my sentience, I felt pain as we passed through some kind of barrier.

Had we left Caer Sidi?

Goddess be cursed, I hoped not. The place I'd viewed as a prison meant safety. Maybe Arianrhod hated me, but at least she'd taken care of me.

"The bitch is still awake," someone warned.

"So's the other one."

I shook my fuzzy head. Inhaling vomit fumes wasn't helping. What other one? I'd asked that question before.

You have to stay awake, a sharp inner voice nagged.

What do you know? Fuck off, I shot back. I might lack telepathy, but answering myself didn't pose any problems.

Very well. Have it your way, but don't say I didn't warn you.

About what?

My thoughts jumped around like a game of checkers gone bad.

Where was I? Who'd kidnapped me? Where was I going? Had I imagined everything? Worse, had the food been poisoned?

Handy way to get rid of me, but Father would figure it out.

I was sobbing again, snot mingling with puke. I felt like crap.

The sour smell deepened. My battle to remain conscious became laughable. Because I had no choice, I gave up and invited darkness to take me. At least it would be a break from the rancid mess I'd turned into. With the last of my awareness, I remembered the warning to stay awake, but it was too late.

I plunged headlong into a chasm lined with my own despair.

CHAPTER 9
ABRIA

I'd exercised the restraint of a saint in Underhill. It had taken everything in me not to throw myself at the two goddesses, swinging and punching until I broke bones in their patrician faces. Magic will never, never replace the satisfaction of a scrappy street brawl.

Maybe I should have waited for Blake, but the more of us who were out hunting for Tiana, the better our chances. At least it seemed that way to me. Ceridwen hadn't been able to locate her via the cauldron. If I let myself dwell on that pithy little fact, I'd have been immobilized.

If a Celtic goddess, and their seer to boot, couldn't find my daughter, what hope would there be for someone like me?

"I cannot think like that," I muttered.

My heart sat in my chest like a stone; my throat was dry. My eyes ached with unshed tears I refused to give in to. I had the whole of eternity to cry. What I needed now was focus, not petty self-indulgence.

My spell was sloppy. I'd aimed for Cailleach's beach, but the place I came out was nowhere near it. A shore, to be sure, but not the one I'd wanted. Sea birds whirled, circled, and headed straight for me. Seals waddled out of the surf. They were as good a place to begin as any.

A pack of rats beat everyone to me, chittering and rubbing against my ankles. Their nearness reminded me I was scarcely dressed for traveling in fancy high-heeled leather boots and a long skirt.

The rodents' group mind surrounded me with love and devotion. They sensed I wasn't myself. A gull landed on one shoulder, talons gripping the inadequate fabric of my top and ripping it. The sun was out, but a chill breeze cut right through me. I didn't bother wasting power to warm myself. Maybe I'd think better if I was uncomfortable.

The first seal reached me and batted my thigh with a flipper as he brushed his slimy snout along my hip. I waited until the rest joined him along with a fat old walrus, whiskers bristling and coated with barnacles.

"I am on a mission," I told them. "The most critical undertaking of my life."

A chorus of, "We will help, mistress," rose from every throat.

"Thank you for your unswerving commitment. My daughter, Tiana, is missing, and—"

A cacophony of hoots, caws, and squeals of outrage drowned out my words. Once the throng quieted, I went on.

"Please, pass the word to all your kin far and wide to be on the lookout for her. She carries my blood, mine and Blake's, so she will be easy to identify."

The walrus crinkled his nose. "Did she run away?"

I shook my head. "She was taken by fell forces from under Arianrhod's very nose."

"But Caer Sidi is impregnable," a gull shrilled.

"So we thought," I agreed. "Whoever has her is powerful."

"What should we do if we see her?" a rat asked.

I thought about her question. "Do not put yourselves in danger," I cautioned. "Call for me through the link I share with each of you. Goddess willing, I'll be near enough to respond."

"What if you're not?" a seal spoke up.

"Find a bird," the gull on my shoulder advised. "We will fly swift and sure to Underhill."

I stroked his feathery side. "Thank you."

"Is there aught else we need to know?" He leaned in to my touch.

"No. Travel swift, sure, and safe. I must spread the word far and wide. With all of you on my side, we shall succeed."

The animals took up my optimistic battle cry. Amid shouts and hoots of "succeed" and "success," the crowd around me dispersed, leaving me alone staring at breakers crashing on the rocky shore.

Determined to do better next time, I took time with my journey spell and visualized Cailleach's stretch of coastline. I'd told Blake I was going to start with the wolf den, but this made far more sense. The odds of Tiana being with the wolves were nil.

This time, my casting ran true. The damp sand and sentinel rocks marking Cailleach's realm shaped up around me. Not surprisingly, the witch goddess stood on the shore. Swinging her attention my way, she barked, "What took you so long?"

Half a head taller than me with a spare, bony build, she had pronounced cheekbones, a high forehead, and a squared-off chin. A beak of a nose dominated her rough features. Tangled silver hair hung to her knees. Dressed in one of her many robes—this one a faded blue—she looked like witches portrayed in children's books.

She is the closest thing I'll ever have to a mother. The temptation to throw myself into her arms was strong, except they weren't open. I gathered my ragged emotions into some semblance of order and walked to her.

"Bad news travels fast," she observed. "I've been expecting you for half an hour."

"Who told you?" I latched onto her dark gaze hoping for solace, for her to tell me this wasn't as bad as I feared.

"Arianrhod and Ceridwen. I asked you a question, child."

My cheeks heated despite the chill of the day and my too-thin garments. "I aimed for here, but ended up...elsewhere."

Her gray brows knitted into a thick line. "Define elsewhere."

"Another bit of beach to the north. It was my own fault. So long as I was there, I requested aid from the animals who came to greet me."

Breath huffed from her making clouds in the air. "A better answer than evil diverting you."

"Who do you think took her?" I blurted.

Cailleach dropped a hand onto my shoulder. "Och, child, would that I knew. I have no idea."

"I still think we should return to Caer Sidi. Surely, there are some clues. No one is powerful enough to sneak in and out without leaving a trace."

"Blake went there with Hedrek. The unicorns are on their way here."

Unicorns. It reminded me of the rest of the animal kingdom. Where were the seals and birds native to this beach? And the mer-people.

"Everyone is hunting Tiana," Cailleach explained in response to my thoughts. "I sent them to search."

"Does *everyone* include the forest dwellers?"

The winter witch goddess nodded.

"Do you think she's off world? Ceridwen couldn't see crap in that kettle of hers."

Cailleach twisted her mouth into a moue. "That one thinks she's a better seer than she is. Long ago, her power ran truer. Something interrupted it."

I didn't care for the sound of that. "Any idea what?"

She nodded slowly. "Aye. She and the Morrigan shared power. When the Battle Crow was imprisoned between Fire Mountain and Satan's realm, she took a portion of Ceridwen's enchantment with her."

"She never mentioned it," I mumbled.

"She wouldn't," Cailleach replied. "She's proud, that

one. Like all the Celts, she'd rather die than admit weakness."

"I still think she should have said something," I sputtered, feeling put out. I'd believed her assessment, and it had stripped hope from me, something I was still fighting to regain.

"You can't change them," Cailleach said pointedly. "Be glad they're assisting."

"But they're who lost track of her." My tone was shriller than I'd have liked.

"You won't change them," she repeated. "They started out convinced Tiana had somehow ensorcelled Roya into forging an escape."

"Until they discovered Roya didn't possess that kind of power," I said bitterly. "Did Arianrhod mention she'd stripped Tiana of her magic?"

Cailleach's eyes widened. "No, she neglected to highlight that."

My mouth tasted of ashes, dry and bitter. "She did release it."

"I see. We can only hope it finds its way back to her."

"Why wouldn't it?" Damn. My too-shrill tone was back.

The witch goddess's grip on my shoulder tightened. "Remember your studies, child. Power removed from its owner has a limited lifespan. Tiana's magic could wither before it finds her. If it does, what she recoups will be a pale shadow of her former ability."

My temper has never been my friend. Fury scoured me, replacing desolation. Suddenly, the day was no longer too cold for comfort, but too warm. I shook off Cailleach's hand.

"Arianrhod must have known. Did she mean to leave Tiana without resources?"

"I'm certain she planned for a short time span, one that wouldn't result in lasting harm."

I knew Cailleach well. I'd trained under her careful eye for over two years. "What aren't you saying?" I demanded.

"Magic requires its owner to regenerate itself. Tiana's power will do its best to locate her, but each dead end will deplete it. There will come a time when no more energy exists, and it will be absorbed by the nearest magical source, good or bad."

"I can't go there," I gritted.

"Then don't. If we give up before we even begin, we're finished."

Stark words, but what I needed to hear. I squared my shoulders. Inactivity grated. We needed to do something, not just stand here.

Hoofbeats pounded against sand. I never saw a portal, but a dozen unicorns galloped toward us, horns gleaming in the sun. Becca was in the lead. She skidded to a stop next to us and laid her horn on my shoulder. The rest of the herd formed a circle around where we stood.

They're the executioners of the magical world. One blow from their horns can end even the most immortal of lives. They're both feared and revered, but Becca and I had forged a special relationship. She's been with me through many battles.

I wrapped an arm around her neck. "Thank you for coming."

"How could I not?" she whinnied. "Your spawn is in

trouble." After a pause, she added, "This might be exactly what she needs to…"

"Shape up and recognize the error of her ways." I supplied helpfully.

"Aye. Good you recognize it."

"I'm not blind to her shortcomings, but let's focus on getting her back. Once she's safe, we can all work harder at corralling her behavior."

"We need to address this methodically." Cailleach was all business.

I'd moved past my inane need for comfort. Perhaps the cold had settled my tattered thoughts. Of course we'd find her. How could we not with so many searching?

Crap. I was a mess. One minute I was certain she was lost to darkness, the next I was equally sure we'd locate her.

Live in the now, an inner voice commanded.

Becca and Cailleach had been talking, but I missed what was said.

"Sorry," I cut in. "What are we doing?"

"We're heading to Caer Sidi," the unicorn informed me.

Enchantment shimmered in the marine air encompassing us all. I let the group spell take me. If we ran into Blake and Hedrek, all good and well. If they'd left, even better because it meant they'd found a clue worth following.

If they could locate it, so could we.

When Becca's magic cleared, we stood on another beach, this one much colder. Sleet shot from gunmetal skies, adding to ice crusting every rock in sight. My teeth began chattering; I funneled a small channel of magic to warm myself.

With my eyes narrowed against the crushing wind and sharp bits of sleet, I looked for the telltale rock marking the entrance to Caer Sidi. Another blast of unicorn power swept me onto Becca's back. Merciful warmth floated upward from her hairy hide. I lay against her neck and wove my arms around it. She knew the way.

No one needed me.

Not true. The same inner voice that had advised me to not get too far ahead of the game had returned. *Your daughter needs you.*

I felt like answering back. Informing my guide or conscience or whoever the hell was chatting with me, Tiana hadn't needed me since she was five years old.

Except it wasn't true.

She'd put up a good show of independence, but she'd crawled into my lap many times when life threw curveballs her way, her sobs heartrending.

We passed through a particular boulder masking one of the ways into Arianrhod's realm. No more sleet. No more wind. It was still cold, but manageable.

Cailleach stood in the inner gateway, the last barrier before Caer Sidi's front entrance. "We must be cautious not to obliterate clues," she warned.

"It means not all of us," Becca told her herd.

I landed lightly on the ground determined to not make things worse.

"Abria?" Blake's deep voice called out.

"She's here," Cailleach replied, "along with me and the unicorns."

Blake's lean form swung into view. Unlike me, he was

dressed for anything, but his feet were bare, presumably to ensure he didn't trample on some choice bit of intel.

I hurried to his side and gripped a wrist. "You're still here. Must mean you haven't found anything."

"Not yet," Hedrek hooted as he flew toward me.

"We're being thorough," Blake explained.

"Let me look," Becca whinnied. "Me and one other unicorn. Our sense of smell is better than yours."

"Our magic is too." A black unicorn neighed derisively.

"None of that." Becca's tone was sharp. She tapped another silver unicorn on its butt with her horn. "Come with me."

The two of them trotted past Blake. The black unicorn was mumbling under his horsey breath. No doubt something about what a waste of time it was to do favors for inferiors.

Hedrek had been scribing circles in the air above us. He wheeled and followed the unicorns.

"Did you find anything at all?" I asked Blake.

"Nay. Whoever was here not only scrubbed evidence of their presence but of everyone else who's been here over the last several years. I've never seen such a clean doorway."

It wasn't good news.

"We'd only combed about half the area, though," he added.

"Did you look for her?" I demanded. "For evidence of her passing?"

"Why?" he countered. "She passed through this portal along with Arianrhod, Roya, and Hedrek scant hours before she was taken. My magic isn't discerning enough to determine if she was coming or going."

A sharp whinny from Becca brought me at a dead run.

"Blood." Her horn pointed at a miniscule flake of something crimson on the wooden porch spanning the entry into Caer Sidi.

Bending her graceful neck, she snaked out her tongue and licked the mini drop. Her equine features churned in disgust; she hacked out saliva.

I waited, my chest tight with fear.

Blake stood next to me, clutching my hand. Like me, he waited for Becca's assessment.

"Leviathan," she neighed. "And this. It's Roya's and was buried between the boards." She extended her tongue. Balanced on its end was a tooth.

"Roya must have bit the monster to leave us something." Blake's words were pained.

"She did well," Cailleach intoned.

I knew next to nothing about Leviathans, so I asked, "Where do they live?" and readied myself. Now that we'd identified who had Tiana, we could go there.

"Not sure. They used to be part of dragonkind, but somewhere along the line they came to represent one of the four crown princes of Hell," Blake said slowly. "Water and a westerly direction are their hallmark."

"I thought Satan had way more princes. And what good does water and west do?" Not the most diplomatic thing to say, but my kid's survival was at stake.

"He does now," Cailleach inserted. "Things were

different long ago. Leviathans are ancient. I didn't know they could operate outside of water."

"Where do they live?" I pressed since no one had exactly answered me.

Blake plucked Roya's tooth from the unicorn and tucked it into a pocket. "The dragons will know where to find them."

"Aye, but whoever came here might have been rogue elements, not associated with the rest of them," Cailleach cautioned.

"Do you have a better idea?" Blake rounded on her before muttering, "Sorry."

"Aye, I do." The witch goddess looked askance at him and turned to me. "Have you consulted the ley lines?"

My cheeks grew hot for a second time. "No, but I should have done that straightaway."

I climbed to the top step, the one right in front of Arianrhod's wooden door. Adorned with runes, its power was palpable and comforting. After sinking into a crouch, I shut my eyes and resurrected my connection with the lines. I hadn't known if they'd be accessible to me from here, but they surrounded me with warmth.

"Do you know where Tiana is?" I asked. No reason to beat around the bush.

"Nay, but we will look. Wait there."

The lines span this world and others. So far, they'd not shared magic with my daughter, wisely determining she lacked the wisdom—or restraint—to manage their bounty.

I didn't have to wait long before, *"Beyond the last circle of Hell,"* whispered through my mind.

"Somewhere past the Ninth Circle?" I sought clarification. *"Is it still on Earth?"*

"Aye and nay."

"Can you help me rescue her?"

"Our power is weak there, but we will not desert you."

As quickly as they'd materialized, they were gone. I rose and faced everyone. "They say she's beyond the last circle of Hell and their magic is weak there."

Blake's expression, Becca's dispirited whinny, and Hedrek's low hoots said it all. My stomach cramped into a hard knot.

"But we know where she is," I insisted. "There must be a way to get there."

"We'd be better off luring them out," Cailleach pronounced.

"Even with the full force of the Sidhe army," Blake said, "we'd lose over half fighting our way to the Ninth Circle. No one has ever explored what lies beyond it."

I closed my teeth over my lower lip, biting hard. "At least we know Satan is behind this."

"Nay, child, 'tisn't clear at all," Cailleach muttered.

"Many wicked things abide in his domain," Blake clarified. "He doesn't pay much heed to who comes and goes so long as they're steeped in evil." A hollow breath rattled from him. "I still say one of us should consult with the dragon council. Leviathans were once part of them."

"They still are," Cailleach said, "which means they will be forced to accept responsibility for their errant kinsmen."

"It's the one thing we can't kill," Becca said.

"Anything dragonesque," another unicorn added.

And the good news just kept piling up...

I'd sent my animal minions on the wildest of wild goose chases. I needed to call them off. Before that, we needed a plan.

Blake turned to Cailleach, "Would you come to Fire Mountain with me?"

"With us." I clattered down the stairs to his side.

After a long pause, the witch goddess said, "Aye, but they may not allow us on their world. It's been closed to all but their kind for longer than my memory."

"We will retreat to our world," Becca said.

"We maintain lore books," another unicorn tossed out. "They may hold pertinent information."

"I will tell the animals they can quit looking," Hedrek volunteered. "But no matter what I say, they will continue their search."

"We have a blueprint for our next steps." Blake's voice cracked revealing his worry. "Everyone will meet back at Underhill in two days' time."

I sent a silent prayer winging to whatever deities took pity on wretches and fools that Tiana's magic had found her. On that cheerful note, I joined my power with Blake's and Cailleach's.

"This will be a long journey," Blake cautioned.

"And far from a pleasant one," Cailleach seconded. "Why didn't you dress for travel, child?"

Because I'm worried sick, rattled, and not thinking straight...

"Didn't expect to be gone all that long," I said stiffly.

The deep velvet of a travel channel swirled and sucked us into its maw. In spite of everything, I was excited to see the dragons' ancestral home. They were animals, albeit magical ones. Would they revere me or view me as a bit of trash to jettison from their world?

Guess I'll find out real soon.

Sagging against Blake, I settled in to wait out the journey.

CHAPTER 10
TIANA

Every muscle, every bone, every cell ached. Even my teeth hurt. I was still encased in the putrid woolen blanket, but it felt different. Looser, somehow.

I started to wriggle, testing if I was still bound, but stilled instantly.

Was anyone here? So long as they believed I was unconscious, they'd leave me alone. At least they had so far.

I thought.

Tales of children sold into slavery and used for unspeakable acts jabbed me. A quick check of my puke-splattered clothing was reassuring. No one had unbuttoned anything. I stank so badly, who'd want to?

I reached outward to test my surroundings. See if anyone else was here. Crap. Relying on magic was second nature. Except Arianrhod had taken it. Damn her to everlasting hell.

Don't get mad, get even.

And do not waste one shred of energy feeling sorry for yourself.

I unclenched my jaw. Two choices. Stick it out in the soiled blanket, or see if I could escape its folds. I stilled my heart, barely breathing, and focused all my attention on gathering clues.

Someone else was near. From the cadence of its breathing, I was almost certain it was Roya. So that was what they'd meant by "the other one."

What to do?

Sooner or later someone would show up and rip the blanket off me. If anyone else was nearby, they were the most quiet breathers in the universe.

Or vampires…Who don't breathe at all.

Sick of second-guessing everything, I pushed my arms in front of me and flung them upward. The blanket flew over my head, splattering me with residual puke.

Fine. It wasn't going to make me any less repellant than I already was.

My eyes flitted this way and that as I worked to absorb as much as I could. Another blanketed lump nearby had to be Roya. Before I woke her, I absorbed our surroundings. We were in a small, dank cave perhaps five meters around and so low my head almost hit the ceiling. Burning torches were stuck into sconces across from each other. The ground was damp dirt with the occasional rock sticking up. I didn't see anything like a doorway.

Big surprise. Whoever had left us here didn't want us to waltz out. Did they know my magic was gone? If not, I'd have to play it very cool and not let on how helpless I was.

Dark water reeking of sulfur ran down the walls.

Wouldn't be drinking that crap no matter how thirsty I became. Wouldn't use it to wash myself off, either.

My heart thudded against my ribcage. I sucked air hard and understood there wasn't all that much here.

After a couple of steadying half breaths—it wasn't as bad if I didn't expect too much—I catalogued what I knew.

We had to be off world.

I held up another finger for the longest time before dropping it. I didn't know anything else, nothing that would assist us in escaping.

A low moan issued from the other blanket.

Guilt seared me. I should have freed her straight away.

Feeling more like 1200 than twelve, I staggered to where she lay and fell onto my knees. It was simple to get a grip on the blanket and tug it out from under her.

Breath whooshed from me; my eyes widened until the muscles around them hurt. Bruises covered every visible inch of flesh. Roya hadn't gone down without a fight.

Where had Arianrhod been?

Did she have any idea a mega battle had played out under her very nose?

I doubled up a fist and punched the air. What the hell use was magic of her magnitude if it didn't warn about danger?

Roya breathed in little panting groans. Her eyes were shut. I stroked her abraded face. "You have to wake up."

She turned away from my touch, moaning louder.

Her condition shocked me; guilt followed on its heels. She was in this mess because of me.

Well, technically, because of her loyalty to Father, but the net result was one and the same. I tried again. "Roya. You have to wake up. They'll be back soon."

Dark eyes flew open. She squealed and clambered to a sit, wincing against the pain movement caused. Tears sheened her eyes. She blinked them away and shivered.

It was cold in here, but that was the least of our problems.

"Do you know where we are?" I asked. When she shook her head, I tried again. "Who took us?"

Her lip curled displaying a broken-off tooth. "Leviathans, except they employed human glamours."

I culled through my memory banks. Monsters had been the topic of some of my lessons. "Aren't they some sort of dragon?" I ventured.

Roya pushed the rest of the blanket off her and nodded. "But I'd bet my last pound note these ones have no affiliation with their kinsmen."

"Then, who are they working for?"

She shrugged. "The critical part is getting out of here." Power crackled around her as she investigated our surroundings, probing for information.

Because my gaze was glued to her face, I didn't need words to confirm we were in very deep shit. Her magic guttered and died, but she remained silent.

"Tell me," I commanded but softened my request by adding, "please."

"We're deep in Hell, deeper than I imagined possible. None of the landmarks I'm familiar with are anywhere close."

My throat, already chafed from being sick and thirsty, went even drier. "Can you teleport us out of here?" I already knew the answer, but I had to ask.

Roya shook her head. "Even if I had that kind of reach, this cave is shielded with something that defeats much of my enchantment."

I rocked back on my heels. "What do they want with us?"

"Not us. You. My suspicion is they want to use you as some kind of bargaining chip."

"For what?"

Roya blew out a weary sounding breath and explored her damaged face with an equally damaged stump. "Your mother is an attractive acquisition because of her link with the ley lines..." Her mouth rounded into an O. "Do you—"

I cut her off with a head shake. "The lines never warmed to me. I tried. They rebuffed me every time." A swallow turned into a convulsion as my parched throat rebelled. Bile splashed the back of my throat.

How could anything be left in my stomach?

"Too bad," she muttered. "And Arianrhod took your magic, so no help from that quarter."

"I'm sorry," I blurted.

I expected her to tell me it was all right, not my fault like everyone else always did. Instead, she set her lips in a thin line. "You should be. If you hadn't been such a brat, neither of us would be here."

Hot words simmered in the back of my throat. They burned, but I held them in. She was right. The truth hurt, but I'd better get used to looking it in the eye.

"Too bad I don't get do overs," I mumbled.

She waved her stumps in my direction. "Same thing I've thought a time or two." Rolling onto her wrists and knees, she pushed upright and made her way to the nearest wall. Once there, she walked along it, poking and prodding.

I had no idea what she was about; it didn't appear useful adding to a possible exit plan.

"Tiana!"

Rather than answer, I hurried to where she stood. At first, I didn't get it, but then the clean smell of fresh water blasted me. I dove in, helping her move rocks out of the way until a small trail of decent water slithered down the wall.

She stood back, but I pushed her forward. "You first. You have all those cuts to clean."

While Roya sluiced the worst of the dirt and grime from her wounds, I debated removing my clothes. It would be just my luck to be buck naked when our captors returned.

"Go ahead and drink," she said and removed her outer garments before continuing to clean herself.

I did. The water was cold and sweet. It might be poisoned, but I didn't care. My poor throat soaked up the liquid and begged for more. Eventually, Roya was done. She'd removed her tunic, wrung it out, and added it to her stack of folded garments.

I settled for washing vomit off my hands, face, and hair. The stench remained, but it wasn't as thick and cloying.

"Better." Roya managed a weak smile.

"Much," I agreed. Were any animals here? If so, they hadn't hustled to my side in a show of solidarity.

"They wouldn't," Roya spoke up. "They're drawn to your magic, and it's dead."

Ugh. Harsh words, but this was my new normal. I didn't rebuke her for reading my mind. If I still had magic, I'd have been using it too.

Roya began awkwardly piling rocks over our water source. I helped. Surely, if our captors knew we had water, they'd find a way to pollute it, make it unusable.

"What now?" I asked, brushing dirt off my hands.

"We wait. Come over here." She settled on a flat span of dirt that wasn't as wet as the rest of the cave floor. I joined her. She was about an hour into telling me the history of the Sidhe, a story I knew and loved, when something shifted.

It didn't require magic to sense when it was nearby even if I couldn't tell who it belonged to.

Roya shot me a look that said to hold still and not give anything away as her voice droned on.

A gleaming black portal formed in the damp air. Before it quit pulsing, a man stepped through. He rubbed his hands together as he looked first at Roya and then at me. "Settling in nicely, girls?"

"I've had worse," Roya sneered.

"Bet she hasn't." The man jerked a long-nailed thumb in my direction. "Spoiled brat princess. She cries at the drop of a wing feather."

I started to my feet, intent on scratching his eyes out.

"Sit!" Roya thundered. The word was laden with compulsion, and I obeyed. A relatively new experience for me.

Laugher rolled from the man. He was tall, about

Father's height, but broader through the shoulders. Leather trousers hung low on his hips. His torso was bare. Reddish hair spilled past his shoulders in a tangled mess. Odd amber eyes with whirling pupils sat above slanted cheekbones. His square chin was dotted with stubble, and his feet were bare.

The same odor from the blankets clung to him. Like something sour that had sat in the sun too long.

"We require food," Roya informed him.

"You may get some, so long as you're not picky," the man agreed.

"Why are we here?" I blurted, determined not to let him cow me.

"You'll find out in due time. Meanwhile, return to whatever it was you were doing."

The same dark portal hovered in the air behind him. He stepped through and was gone.

"Was he the same one who took us?" I kept my voice low in case he was close enough to hear and got back to my feet.

"Aye. Leviathan wearing a glamour." Roya stood too.

Anger surged. If I had my way, I'd cut off his balls and feed them to Hedrek. My arms were outstretched. Lightning shot from my fingertips, residual fury running amok. I stared, not daring to hope it meant what I thought it did.

Was it residual power? Or was my magic back online?

Roya stared, naked hope sheening her eyes. *"Can you hear me?"*

A smile stretched my mouth wide as it ever got. *"Yes! Yes I can."*

Beyond hope, my power was restored. For good

measure, I opened myself to its flow and relished how it filled the spots I'd been hollow.

"How?" I asked Roya.

She leaned close to my ear. "Arianrhod must have released it, and it was hunting you. All it needed was a chink in the barrier around this cave. When the Leviathan opened a portal—twice—it gave your power precisely the opportunity it sought."

My heart pounded; my temples throbbed. I was whole again. Thanks be to every god or goddess who'd ever walked.

"Maybe I can get us out of here." Unlike Roya, I didn't bother to whisper.

"Ssht." She grabbed my arm hard enough to hurt. "We cannot push power through the blockade around this place. Our only hope is for them to let us out of here. Then, and only then, can we make our move."

"But—"

"No buts." She squeezed harder. "If Arianrhod could remove your power, so can this bunch. Pretend to be docile, browbeaten. They'll let their guard down sometime, and we'll be gone."

I started to laugh.

"What in the hell is so funny?" Her tone could have cleaved granite.

"It's the same strategy I planned to employ to escape from Caer Sidi."

"Really?" Roya arched a russet brow. "You'd have made me look bad."

"Sorry."

She still clutched my arm. "You have to begin thinking about someone beyond yourself, child."

I started to argue but gave it up before even a single word emerged. "Yeah. You're right."

A surprised look washed over her thin, pointed features. Turning, she returned to where we'd been sitting and picked up a rock with a sharp side. Twisting it to an optimal angle, she began drawing runes in the dirt.

I sat close enough to read them. Finding a rock of my own, I added to her plan in a few places. She was mapping out how we'd escape if an opportunity presented itself.

Once we were done, she erased each rune, taking care to subvert the bit of magic powering it. "We have a plan," she said softly.

Indeed we did.

For the first time since we'd been captured, I let myself hope the remainder of my very long life wouldn't unfold in the backside of Hell, or wherever Roya had said we were.

Magic was our ticket out of here. Mine and Roya's. Together we could do this. I vowed to Danu and the universe that if I got out of this mess, I'd be a whole new person. High-handed Tiana was a thing of the past. It would take time and commitment, but I'd be the daughter my parents had hoped for.

Roya's stump covered one of my hands.

"Never forget that vow," she said solemnly. "Hold it before you like a beacon."

"I will."

Talk is cheap. But I had to do better. If I hadn't been such a ninny, I wouldn't be here, wouldn't have put Roya's existence at risk along with my own. Goddess only knew how many Sidhe and animals were beating the bushes hunting me.

Suddenly, I felt cheap and small. And ashamed. Why hadn't Mother and Father taken me to task more often?

They tried. I made it pretty damned impossible...

The initial glow at being whole again was fading, not because I wasn't thrilled, but because I was exhausted. Rolling onto my side, I cradled my head in my arms and shut my eyes. For a while, I drifted, but then I slept. In my dreams, animals surrounded me offering love and support.

I opened my arms, and they crawled into them.

BLAKE

My estimate regarding travel time was woefully optimistic, and I'd said the journey would be long. Abria drowsed as she leaned against me; Cailleach muttered under her breath in a language I couldn't quite make out.

"Have you been there before?" she asked.

I wove a calming spell around Abria, hoping she'd remain asleep. The dark circles scribed beneath her eyes and new lines in her forehead spoke to her exhaustion and deep worry about our daughter.

"Aye," I answered Cailleach, "but not for several hundred years. I don't imagine the place has changed."

"How could it have?" She scrunched her strong-boned face into a resigned expression. "Do you suppose they'll allow us into the caves?"

"What you're really asking is if they'll grant us an audience," I clarified. "I have no idea, but it costs us nothing to try."

"Time. It costs us time."

"Not really. Storming the gates of Hell's deepest circle will require more than a Sidhe army."

She arched steel-gray brows. "You're hoping the dragons will pick up the slack and go after their fallen kinsmen?"

When I heard it out loud, I recognized how truly remote it was. "Aye and nay. They will have ideas. Certainly, they'll know which of their ilk is behind this. They may even know why." I stopped for a moment, collecting my thoughts.

"Dragons have a shared consciousness," she murmured. "I'm not sure it extends to those who've left the fold permanently, but it may. Right now, we have very few options to reclaim Tiana. If things go well, we'll be better armed when we leave Fire Mountain. If not, we cannot reclaim the time this side trip will have cost us."

"Might not cost us all that much. You do realize their, erm, greeting party, may send us packing," I murmured.

"They've always heard me out, even if they didn't invite me in out of the sun." Cailleach snorted but didn't add to her opinion with further words.

Fire Mountain is a desolate place. Hot and dry, its winds blow continually, making the place feel like a bake oven. Sand swirls and blows, abrading any bit of exposed skin. The land is circled by a ring of active volcanoes that take turns spewing magma and lava. They flow across the sand in burning rivers that take a long while to cool. I'd learned the hard way to steer clear of them.

An extensive cave system has a single entrance. It winds

deep beneath the surface with much cooler temperatures and a magnificent spring partway down yielding crystal-clear cold water. The spring must spawn underground rivers that break through somewhere because herds of wildebeest roam on the far side of the ring of volcanoes providing both food and sport for the dragons.

In an oddly symbiotic relationship, the dragons were both herdsmen and executioners. They must care for the wildebeests or they'd have been hunted to extinction long since.

"Watch your spell!"

Cailleach's sharp words snapped me back to attention. My journey spell was, indeed, winding down. It was at the point where I needed to shape it, encourage it to penetrate the barrier around the dragons' world. I did my part and waited.

"Are we almost there?" Abria asked. She still sounded tired, but at least she'd rested through the transit.

"Almost," I said and hoped I was right. The dragons always posted sentries, and they were perfectly capable of shoving my enchantment off the rails. I'd never understood why they deployed the manpower for 24/7 surveillance. Surely, there couldn't be that many visitors. If the odd undesirable broke through, they were imminently capable of dispatching them.

Not my responsibility.

Hell, I couldn't even corral the Sidhe on some days. How could I possibly have a handle on managing dragons?

A shudder ran through our pod. The distinctive reek of reptile, scales baking under a relentless sun, surrounded us.

Dragon enchantment blasted through me. I left myself open beneath their inquiry. Far better if they didn't think I had something to hide.

With zero warning, our enclosure shattered, leaving us to tumble toward sand stretching far below. Heat blasted me, searing my throat and dragging every shred of moisture out of my mouth and nose. I broke my fall with a cushion of hot air.

Abria beat me to the ground. Cailleach touched down behind me and tugged at the neck of her robe. "Never get used to this," she mumbled.

No one ever "got used to" this level of heat. Except the dragons.

A large black female winged toward us. I stood tall and waited until she plopped down a meter away. Sand sprayed up from her bulk, peppering my face with hot bits.

"I am Nymeria. State your reason for violating our borders."

Mmph. They'd formalized their interrogation. She knew damned good and well who all of us were, but I'd play along. I bowed, not low but halfway. "I am Elwyn Cardassier, prince of the Sidhe. With me are Cailleach, winter witch goddess, and Abria, animal mage, daughter to the ley lines, and my mate."

"I asked why you are here. I already know who all of you are." Her tone was chilly, if anything could be the least bit cold here.

So she had.

I nodded, neglected to apologize, and said, "Leviathans

kidnapped our daughter. Since they are part of your kinship circle, Fire Mountain seemed a logical place to—"

"Your daughter is not here. May shame fall upon your house if you'd believe for a moment we'd harbor a Sidhe against her will. Begone." Nymeria made flapping motions with both forelegs.

"We know Tiana isn't here." Abria stepped closer to the dragon. She'd opened the neck of her shirt; sweat sheened her skin and dampened her hairline.

Nymeria lowered her head, sniffing audibly as she absorbed Abria's unique scent. Her tongue snaked out, and she licked droplets of sweat. Once Abria's forehead was dry, the dragon arched her neck and dropped her head on Abria's shoulder.

"You will remain with us," she pronounced.

Cailleach held up a hand and growled, "She does not belong to you."

The dragon hissed, shooting a small tongue of flame at the witch. "What do you know? This is none of your affair."

"Aye but it is." Cailleach stepped closer and placed a hand on the dragon's broad snout. "I schooled this mage and claim rights over her."

"We would provide far more comprehensive training." The dragon came as close to purring as a dragon can.

"I appreciate the offer." Abria's fingers played over the dragon's shiny black scales. "But what I need is assistance locating Tiana."

"It may be possible."

My eyebrows crawled up my forehead. Abria's power over animals extended to dragonkind. I'd never have anticipated that. They wouldn't follow her blindly like her other minions, but from the looks of things, they'd revere her. The dragon's next words clinched my impression.

She lifted her head and said, "Accompany me. We will visit the elders and present your request."

Spreading her wings, Nymeria skimmed along the sand. I followed her lead. My feet were uncomfortably hot from prolonged contact with the sand. Flying fixed that problem. Cailleach and Abria trudged along, keeping up with the dragon's pace.

I'd have carried Abria, but I didn't want to dilute her position in Nymeria's eyes. I'd only been invited into the dragons' caves once—when they'd needed Sidhe cooperation. My other visits had all been conducted on the burning sand in the midst of windstorms.

Not that I could have found my way beneath ground on my own. The dragon led us to a spot in the endless sand that looked and felt just like everywhere else. One moment, it was all sand, the next an opening formed leading downward. Relief from Fire Mountain's triple suns was instantaneous as we dropped beneath ground level.

I wiped sweat off my forehead. The superheated air had dried it almost as quickly as it formed, but I needed water. Soon, we'd pass the spring. I knew better than to help myself.

"May I avail myself of your water?" I asked.

Nymeria didn't even turn around.

"My mate requests water." Abria's clear, ringing voice reverberated off the passageway's walls. She was taking advantage of her animal mage talent being valued.

Two bends in the trail later, the dragon stopped at the spring's entrance. I smelled its freshness before it came into view. The sacred well hadn't changed. Bursting out of iridescent crystals in the middle of pink and green rocks, its rushing hum was mesmerizing as water clattered over a precipice on its way to points unknown.

All of us drank, including Nymeria, before she herded us ever lower. I swear, the dragons had excavated more passageways since my last sojourn here.

Or maybe they'd altered my memories so I couldn't describe the way to anyone else.

Regardless, eventually we turned into a huge chamber with a podium far below and rows of benches arranged in tiers between it and the doorway. Iridescent lichen clinging to the walls provided light. Four dragons stood behind the dais at the lowest point of the room. I'd met all of them before.

The group included two white dragons flanking Nidhogg and Dewi, the Norse and Celtic dragons. Nidhogg was coal black, Dewi blood-red. The two white dragons were blind and had served as seers to dragonkind for time out of mind.

Plumes of smoke rose lazily upward. I'd expected the council chamber to be full. Dragons are curious by nature, and I bet visitors were rare as speckled hens' teeth. Not many made it through the gauntlet.

"Been a while," Nidhogg growled.

I hooked an arm into Abria's and nodded at Cailleach to come too. Together, we walked down a very long flight of stairs leading to the dais. I stopped about twenty steps from the bottom, let go of Abria, and bowed low.

"Thank you for your hospitality."

Fire shot from Dewi's jaws. When she opened her mouth, double rows of shiny teeth gleamed in the low light from the lichens. "Why are you here? You must want something, and quite badly."

I nodded pleasantly. "Much the way you wanted something from me when you dragged me here from Underhill."

The fire turned into a veritable blowtorch. Nidhogg jabbed her with a foreleg. "Stop that."

"You can't tell me what to do."

"I am head of this council."

"This time around," Dewi simpered snidely.

What the hell? Did they take turns leading the charge?

Before they took a break to teleport elsewhere and duke it out, I said, "Forgive the intrusion, but—"

"They're here because their daughter was taken," one of the blind seers announced. I've never known either of their names. Now didn't seem the time to ask.

"By Leviathans," the other chimed in.

"Not possible." The look Nidhogg shot at his seer said he'd lost his dragon-esque mind.

The white dragon shrugged amid the clattering of scales. When he moved, it showcased their undersides, which were silver. Unlike the other dragons whose eyes were a rich green rimmed in gold, both seers had milk-white eyes without iris or pupil.

The Norse dragon shuffled around until he faced the seer who'd shrugged. "Why didn't you say something?"

Another shrug, this one noisier than the first. "We do not involve ourselves in other mages' problems."

"But this particular"—Dewi paused long enough to shoot more flame and ash upward—"problem has ramifications."

"Like what?" Both seers bristled and appeared to grow larger. Leathery wings spread wide, fanning the air. In contrast to their bodies, the wings were a delicate pale blue.

This time, Nidhogg pushed fire through his open jaws. "We. Do. Not. Draw. Attention. To. Ourselves. Period." More fire mixed with ash swirled; some settled on me. I hurried to brush it off before it burned holes in my garments.

"Leviathans are not part of us," one of the seers noted.

"Haven't been for some time," the other chimed in.

Tell me something I don't know.

No one was paying attention to me. Good thing since my inner commentary was snarky as fuck. We were guests here. Never mind, we'd skated in on Abria's coattails.

My mate unhooked herself from my hold on her and trudged a few steps lower. "I don't care who is part of what," she announced.

I hustled after her, intent on advising her to modulate her tone, but I was too late.

She forged ahead. "If you know anything at all about your renegade kinsmen that will help Blake and me locate Tiana, I'd very much appreciate hearing it. Time grows short." She tapped her breastbone. "I feel it here. Will you assist us or no?"

Nidhogg turned his attention on her, eyes spinning hypnotically. Lesson number one when dealing with dragonkind was never meet their gaze. They'd spear you like a bug, only freeing you if the spirit moved them.

I stood on the step just above her. Shouting not to look at Nidhogg would paint me as impossibly rude. As a compromise, I dropped a hand on her shoulder and employed what I hoped was private telepathy.

"Don't look at his eyes."

Abria ignored me and faced off against Odin's pet. Probably the way Odin viewed Nidhogg, but certainly not how the dragon viewed his role with the Norse god.

"You came to us," Nidhogg reminded Abria—and probably Cailleach and me as well. "You will remain until we choose to release you."

"Like hell we will." Abria sliced a hand downward and took on a familiar glow as she summoned the ley lines to her side.

"But you belong with us." Dewi's tone was silky. Compulsion rode beneath her statement.

Cailleach skirted around me and positioned herself next to Abria. Visible power flowed between the two women, forming a shimmery gateway off to one side.

Was Cailleach immune to the dragons' mesmerism too? Made me low man on the totem pole since I wanted to throw myself at Nidhogg's scaled hind feet and pledge fealty.

"I belong to no one but myself," Abria announced as she moved her gaze from one dragon to the next. "If you choose that path, we shall leave. You cannot hold us."

The portal brightened, beckoning invitingly. My overwhelming desire to cede agency to the dragons retreated a few paces.

Meanwhile, the seers had moved next to one another. Streamers in the air suggested they were communicating.

"We should do as they request," one of the seers said.

"Why?" Nidhogg asked pointblank.

"Because it is foretold," the other seer added.

"Tells me less than nothing," Nidhogg growled. At least the cavalcade of smoke and ash had slowed.

"What? You're missing the definition of foretold?" Dewi arched both scaled brows.

I winced. Nidhogg rounded on her, and I expected a full-on confrontation. Instead, he bugled. She bugled back until the hall rang with discordant notes beating against one another.

What I don't know about dragons is legion. I'd heard them bugle, but always individually. As if they'd been waiting in the outer hall, scores of dragons shuffled into the chamber, turning this way and that as they plopped onto benches ringing the room.

Dewi extended a wing; Abria's gateway winked out. "We may allow you to leave," she said in her gravelly voice, "but first we will tell you how a small band of Leviathans left our realm."

"Will it be useful in our search for Tiana?" Cailleach asked.

"Perhaps," Nidhogg growled.

"Always valuable to know about your enemies," one of the seers chucked in helpfully.

"What do you think?" Abria's shielded mind speech was garbled.

"Might give us clues where to look."

"But we already know she's beyond the Ninth Circle of Hell."

"I meant to say ideas for how to proceed."

"We can hear you," Nidhogg said dryly. "If you know where she is, why bother us?"

My turn to step up. "We are unsure what we face," I explained. "Traveling that deep into Hell will wipe out a goodly portion of my army. None of us have journeyed beyond the Ninth Gate."

"If we could determine what the Leviathans want with Tiana—" Abria began.

"'Tisn't her they want, but you." A seer corroborated one of my earlier theories.

"Not her, but control over the ley lines," the other seer clarified.

"Why?" Cailleach asked. "What good are ley lines to Leviathans?"

"You ask questions that may be answered once you know more," Dewi replied, punctuating her words with a staunch bugle. It was taken up by a chamber full of dragons and was so loud it was tough not to clap my hands over my ears.

I'd wanted to be gone half an hour ago, but the seer was right about knowledge being power. Dewi and Nidhogg had been certain enough we'd take the bait they'd summoned their minions for story time.

The longer we remained, though, the harder it would be to leave. They didn't have power over Cailleach and Abria yet. Only over me. Was this a gambit to ensure they ended up with Abria—and the ley lines—as a prize?

Not the place to make a mistake, so I extended the slimmest tendril of power intent on accessing at least one dragon mind. At first I targeted a seer, but changed my mind at the last minute and tried Nidhogg. He was arrogant enough, it would be the last thing he'd expect.

"Well?" Dewi crossed her forelegs as she waited for us to make up our minds.

I grabbed the moment to push into Nidhogg's mind but not very far. If he detected me, punishment would be swift and sure. At the least, I'd be summarily ejected from Fire Mountain. To avoid notice, I trod softly, skimming the surface and gathering what I could.

Disquieting images jostled one another. Leviathans burning but not being consumed. The Fire Mountain volcano spewing magma. Arching over everything was desire for Abria, not as a lover but as a possession that would give dragons power over all living creatures.

Unlike her other minions, dragons viewed her as a powerful chip on a cosmic board. The Norse dragon shook his head; I withdrew as quietly as I'd entered. His longing for Abria worried me, but I wanted to hear what he had to say about Tiana's captors.

After rolling my shoulders back and spreading my wings —to remind them they weren't the only ones who had them —I said, "I propose a compromise. Abria feels we must move quickly, yet you hold invaluable information."

I inclined my head at the four directly below. "Dragons are renowned for storytelling. In this instance, if you could limit yourselves to what is directly relevant, we'd appreciate it."

"Yes, we can always return at a later date to hear the full tale," Abria spoke up.

"Five minutes," Cailleach said. "Ten at the most."

I winced, expecting dragonfire to reduce her to a pile of bones. No one dictated to dragonkind. No one.

"But we'd barely be getting started," Dewi protested in the same silken tones.

I cultivated a bland expression to mask my surprise the Celtic dragon goddess had chosen persuasion over violence.

"Make it work, please." I stretched my wings wider.

"Or we'll leave immediately." Abria caught on fast.

Amid grumbling, Nidhogg said, "Very well. In the beginning, dragonkind were comprised of us, sea serpents, and Leviathans, a particular type of serpent who also took human form and walked on land..."

CHAPTER 12
TIANA

Time slithered past. I had no way to judge how much. No windows. No differentiation between day and night. The promised food was slow to arrive. Very slow. It felt as if days had elapsed before the same black portal flared to life disgorging two large rank-smelling bones covered with meat.

Roya rose from what had become her spot in our small cave and inspected the latest arrivals.

I cupped a hand over my nose to reduce the stench while Roya prodded a bone with one foot. When it rolled over, cream-colored, segmented maggots crawled out and headed straight toward me.

Mother may have an affinity for insects. I'd never appreciated them. Still, I forced myself to crouch low and extend my hands in greeting. Small, childlike, inarticulate voices swirled, and the tiny, wormlike creatures crawled up my legs.

These were the first animals I'd seen since my capture. They made me smile. I'd underestimated insects, one of many mistakes I'd do well not to repeat.

"Get ready for more," Roya called and toed the other leg onto its side.

Maggots streamed from it. This batch was on the dark brown side; most were still chewing. Maggots are the cleaners of the animal kingdom. With an uncanny ability to segregate rotten flesh from sound, they've been used on battlefields and in primitive hospitals for hundreds of years.

I'd have known more about them if I'd had a better attitude toward my lessons. Soon, hundreds roved all over me, dipping under my clothing in places. The touch of their mouths wasn't as creepy as I'd anticipated.

Because it had only been Roya and me for so long, I wasn't quick on the uptake. Across the cave from me, she'd piled rocks into a primitive barbeque pit and was busily crafting fire. Given the lack of burnables, her entire cooking effort would require a flow of power.

"Holler if you need help," I said.

She was so intent on her task, she didn't answer. I got it; both of us were half starved. Magic is a picky mistress requiring adequate rest and food to function at peak performance.

Insects aren't warm blooded, but the net effect of all those tiny bodies creeping this way and that was soothing in an unexpected way. And then it hit me. They'd come from outside this cave. Did they hold information that might help us escape?

"Where exactly are we?" was my first shot out of the box.

A chorus of "home" and "here," told me none of them had ever ventured beyond wherever we were. Why would they? Their lifespans are short, measured in days before they turn into flies.

I tried again. *"What is it like beyond this cave?"*

"Bigger and the same," was followed by, *"Hot."*

So far, I was batting dead zero. *"Can we escape?"*

"Why would you want to?"

Finally, something I could respond to, hopefully in terms they'd appreciate. *"I was taken from my family. I miss them."*

Crooning filled my mind. I'd touched a nerve. Unlike some insects that possess a group intelligence, maggots are independent.

"We could ask for you," someone ventured.

"No! Do not do that." I sealed my order with a spell. The last thing we needed was some Leviathan laughing at my paltry efforts to circle the wagons. They might know about Mother, but perhaps my magic was an unknown quantity to them. I wanted to keep it that way.

The best scenario would be for them to believe I had no power at all.

"Tiana." Roya's voice sounded weak, not like her at all.

Maggots and all, I rushed to her side. The meat didn't stink as much cooking as it had raw. Her arms were outstretched. Blood dripped from the stumps feeding the flames she'd created. Her skin had turned the color of old parchment; she swayed on her feet.

"I'll take over. Sit down before you fall down."

She didn't argue as I'd expected but sank into a crouch. I

fiddled with her spell until I had a reasonable flow of heat beneath the bones. Saliva pooled; I spat it out.

"Thanks," Roya murmured.

"Why didn't you call me sooner?"

"Thought I could finish."

My maggot friends slithered from me to Roya, covering her with their tiny bodies. She crooned to them in Gaelic, telling them she welcomed their assistance. The words confused me until I looked at where the bugs settled. They cleaned wounds she'd sustained when we were kidnapped from Caer Sidi.

Despite our efforts with clean water and dribbles of magic, we'd missed a few places infections were brewing. I turned the meat; it was nearly done.

"Mine's good enough," Roya said.

I shook my head. "Nope. We have to be sure it won't make us sick." Adding a few degrees to my efforts, I willed dinner to cook faster. It wasn't much, but anything was better than water, which was all we'd had since our arrival.

Locating a flat rock close to Roya, I instructed the larger of the two bones to settle there. The maggots rearranged themselves so she could eat.

Heedless of being burned, I snatched the second bone from where it had been suspended in the air while it cooked and bit off a chunk. It was tough and flavorless, but at least it no longer smelled of rot. Hunkered over it like a lioness over a prize kill, I chewed and swallowed over and over until nothing but the bare bone remained.

A cracking noise brough my head up. Roya was pounding on the bone with a smallish rock. Of course.

Marrow. In the spirit of leaving nothing edible behind, I did the same, sucked the hollow in the bone, and licked grease from my lips.

The maggots formed a heap next to Roya. They must have run out of things to eat. Some were spinning cocoons preparatory to turning into flies. I crawled closer to Roya. "Better?"

She nodded and turned her dark eyes on me. "We need far more fare than this if we're to have the strength to break free."

"They don't want us strong."

"Aye, but they do want us alive. We're not much use to them dead." She set her lips in a thin line. "This isn't pretty, Tiana, but I'm not much more than collateral damage. Do not be surprised if they separate us, and—"

"Hush. Don't say such things." I threw my arms around her.

She hugged me for a moment; the sweet scents of fairy wafted from her, pleasant and soothing. And then she let go and pushed me an arm's length away. "We must prepare for all eventualities."

The not-yet-digested meat sat in my stomach like a stone. I laced my fingers over my belly urging it to hang onto its contents.

"Your father and mother are hunting for us," she went on. "Like as not Arianrhod and Ceridwen as well. Arianrhod knows good and well this is her fault."

"Not sure it would bother her," I mumbled.

"Neither here nor there. My point is many seek us. All we have to do is hang on. Eventually, someone will show up."

I unclenched my jaw. "Maybe. I wasn't at the top of anyone's favorite person list, not even my parents." The backs of my eyes developed the burning sensation presaging tears. I refused to give into them.

"Don't be absurd." Roya's tone was sharp.

"How about realistic? I know precisely how horrid I was. If it comes down to a choice between me and sacrificing a chunk of the Sidhe army in a rescue attempt, Father may decide on some other route."

"We'll get through this."

I stared at her through a sheen of tears I'd vowed not to allow past the gates.

She took my meaning well enough because she added, "After my human father chopped my hands off, I fell many stories. When he came after me to finish the job, I pretended I was already dead.

Her face twisted in a sour expression. "It was close. I couldn't bind my wounds until he left, but I did employ magic to staunch the flow of blood. He and my uncles had dealt a major blow to Holder's clan, but not without cost. All of my clan lay dead or dying in the manor house.

"Except for him.

"It was why Father left my side and tottered back inside —to see if he could save anyone. Later, much later, I heard his howls of pain and knew he was the only one left. By then, the next night had fallen. I'd patched myself up enough to head for the *Dreaming*. As a parting gift, I cobbled a casting. When Father next walked beneath the lintels and out into the world, it would snare him and make him go mad."

"What does that have to do with us?"

"Never give up hope."

I glanced around our prison. "The situations aren't the same. You weren't trapped a bazillion kilometers from home."

"Och, child, don't be so literal."

Her rebuke stung. I bristled at being called child.

"Difficult situations require creativity and looking beyond them to better days. Besides"—she smiled crookedly—"we're tough to kill."

Flies buzzed above the pile of maggots. Whoa. I'd had no idea their pupa stage was so brief. Perhaps it wouldn't have been if this bunch were normal. These were special Hell-spawned maggots who operated on a singular timetable.

Several circled my head.

"Can you reach the other side?" I asked

"What other side, mistress?"

"The one the meat came from."

The buzzing escalated. Two glowed brightly before vanishing. Hmph. Answered one question. I sprang to my feet, yelling, *"Wait."*

Like all animals of all ilks, they obeyed me. *"Travel to your starting point. Notice what you pass. Then return and tell me."*

Over half the maggots had transitioned to flies. Traveling in a swarm not unlike bees, they flew straight into a wall and disappeared.

Roya lurched upright. "Wonder if they know something we don't," she said and probed the spot the bugs had vanished.

I joined her, illuminating the spot with a mage light.

"Look. There." Roya angled a stump at a spot about a meter below the ceiling.

Walking close, I examined it. Disappointment surged. "It's a hole, but very tiny."

"Maybe we can make it bigger." A dart flew from her, marking the spot.

I replayed our days in the cave. We'd looked for weak spots in the weave holding us in place, but we'd been searching for large rents, not miniscule holes.

"Might be bigger ones we missed earlier," I said.

More maggots completed their transition and flew from our cave. Too bad shapeshifting wasn't one of my skills.

The zing of Leviathan power made the fine hairs at the back of my neck shoot to attention. Roya snagged her dart, burying it in a wall. By the time a portal heaved into view, we stood arm in arm facing it.

My heart pounded; my throat was dry.

"Might just be more food," Roya whispered.

"Doubtful."

The same mage who'd visited us before reappeared. At least he looked the same. Any being who can shapeshift is probably capable of looking however they want.

"I trust you dined well." He glanced pointedly at the bone shards.

I didn't bother answering.

The rest of the maggot pile surged to life. The ones that were flies picked up pupas and flew from the cave.

The Leviathan stared after them. "They're edible too."

"Drat." I snapped my fingers. "How could we have missed them?"

The mage stomped toward us. "Your presence is required...elsewhere."

My fingers dug into Roya's arm. "Where might that be?" she asked.

"You do not get to ask questions." He leaned close until the rotten-fish stench of him became unbearable. My eyes and nose began to run. At least he hadn't made noises about separating us.

"Will we be returning here?" Roya leveled her gaze at him.

"Hard to say."

She pivoted away from me and grabbed the pile of clothing she'd left on a rock. I looked longingly at the place our fountain flowed. If we weren't coming back, who knew when I'd next get a drink of water.

Another portal slammed into view. Two more mages poured out of it. Presumably, these were also Leviathans, but I didn't dare deploy magic to check. Harsh words in a language I didn't recognize flew from the newcomers.

Roya's brows inched up. I might not understand what was said, however she did. Curiosity choked me, but I didn't dare employ mind speech—or anything else. My guess was the first mage hadn't moved fast enough for someone's taste.

The two newcomers stomped toward me. I held my ground, feet spread, chin high. Defiance is where I live, so I didn't have to work hard—or at all—to project exactly what I thought about this shitshow.

Roya bent, put the garment heap on the ground, and pawed through it. When she was done, she handed me a few items and pressed a stump against my wrist. "Remember what we talked about."

I nodded as if I got it, but confusion reigned. Which thing, exactly, did she mean?

Leviathan power surrounded me. I reached for Roya. She shook her head. "They want you by yourself."

One of the mages cackled. "This one is smart."

"We'll see how the other one shapes up," a mage snarked.

My bold posture didn't change, but fear burned a hole in my belly. The only thing that had made this whole mess tolerable was not being alone. I'd played at being independent, but it was easy since I'd had multiple fallback positions.

No longer.

What to do? If I engaged in a full-blown display of power, I'd have tipped my hand. Probably for nothing. Unspoken words raked through my mind. The only ones that made it out were, "Thank you." Little enough to let Roya know how much her presence meant to me.

She held my gaze. "You can do this. You carry the blood of the gods."

Rings of pain closed around me, jabbing so hard I felt faint. I started to shake, but I'd be damned if I'd cry out. The cave dissolved replaced first by stinking blackness, and then by light so bright it hurt my eyes.

Peering through slits, I saw fires, lots of them crackling with unnatural power. The cave hadn't looked much like I'd envisioned Hell, but this sure did. Sweat poured from me in response to heat more intense than anything I'd ever imagined. I'd had plenty to drink from the spring, but I wouldn't stay hydrated long.

Agony shot through my jaw. I'd broken a tooth biting down so hard. My feet burned, heat translating through the too-thin soles of my shoes. The smell of burning flesh terrified me once I understood my body was the culprit.

I can do this. I can do anything. Great, my own internal pep squad in action.

A rough, scaled arm dragged me upright. I hadn't realized I was sunk into a crouch. Opening my eyes a little more, I saw what had to be a Leviathan.

No glamour, the real thing. Impossibly huge and covered with gray scales, it was a cross between dragons I'd seen in books and sea serpents. Six dark-green eyes were scattered randomly on either side of a broad snout. They whirled and spun, but not in any kind of synchrony.

"No matter what happens," burned across my mind, *"you will be ours forever."*

They might require telepathy to communicate. I didn't. "Like hell I will," I shouted before I fell apart.

Screams ripped through me, one after the other until my throat ached, but I couldn't stop. The monster who still had hold of my arm casually backhanded me across the face. Razor-sharp scales cut my skin. Blood flowed.

I was still yelping when the creature's forked tongue snaked out and licked the droplets.

Alarm raced through me. I'd been a shit student, but one

lesson had sunk in. Never, never let an enemy get hold of your blood. If gives them power over you.

Something in the thing's saliva encouraged my blood to flow faster.

I might be done for, but I would not go down without a fight. The next yelp turned into a roar. I had to make this work. I'd never get another chance.

Summoning the power that had always raced to my call, I jerked out of the Leviathan's slimy grip and prepared to make conquering me so unpleasant they'd toss me back into the pit with Roya.

The drab little cavern was looking better and better. At least Roya was safe. If I had anything to say about it, she'd remain so.

CHAPTER 13
ABRIA

I'd never have agreed to a dragon storytelling session. Had Blake lost his ever-loving mind? While not falling over their tails to ingratiate themselves like my other minions, the dragons appeared captivated by me.

I wanted to leverage that fascination, turn it into action and aid. From what Blake intimated, battling our way through Hell would decimate the Sidhe army, and we wouldn't even have gotten to where Tiana and Roya were being held.

And then, there was the problem of how we'd get back. No one was talking about that part of the mission.

I listened to Nidhogg and Dewi drone on with half an ear. So far, they'd covered how Leviathans were formed from a combination of dragon and sea serpent genetics with the added benefit of shapeshifting to whatever form they chose.

Hmmm. So humans were only one of the possibilities.

Blake nudged me in the ribs. He must have sensed my inattention.

"Rather like you," Nidhogg was saying as he pointed a foreleg my way, "our creation didn't come out as we'd hoped."

I bristled. Before I could retort that the two instances had nothing to do with one another, Blake gripped my arm. I clenched my teeth to keep hot words at bay. The Celts had created me as an experiment, one they'd argued over for years thereafter. Long past when I escaped their clutches, they still fell into two camps: those who thought I was a grand idea and those who were convinced they needed to hunt me down and end me.

Not about me. An inner voice held sharp tones.

"Could you hurry things up?" Cailleach stared at the dragons.

"You're free to wait above," Dewi told her.

"I think not," the witch retorted. "You find it tolerable, but 'tis far too hot for anyone who isn't dragonkind."

"Cailleach has a point." Blake stepped in. "We must launch a rescue effort. So far, while your tale is interesting, it hasn't given me anything I can use to help Tiana."

One of the blind seers turned his milky gaze our way. "When they were refused the full rights accorded to dragons, a few Leviathans left Fire Mountain. We haven't seen them in the last"—he narrowed his lidless eyes—"900 years or so."

"How many is a few?" I asked. "And how many Leviathans remained here?"

"Six or seven," the seer replied. "In terms of their

numbers in Fire Mountain, it's zero. None of them wished to stay, so we removed the other forty to a mirrored world where they could self-govern."

"Worked to everyone's benefit," Dewi noted. "We weren't faced with our failures, and they weren't saddled with our disappointment."

"Has anyone checked on them lately?" Blake asked.

Nidhogg's scaled brows shot up. "Why would we?"

"They could have joined forces with Satan or the ones who waltzed out of here." Blake looked pained, as if he were explaining arithmetic to a schoolchild.

"No dragon would ever get within a wing's length of the king of Hell," Nidhogg pronounced.

"Then you won't mind a quick trip to check on your kinsmen," I said. Blake may not have scored points with the dragons, but he had with me. We needed to know what we faced. Was it half a dozen or fifty?

A flurry of wings from the upper reaches of the chamber suggested someone had chosen to do my bidding. I have that effect on animals. The dragons weren't immune.

"Do they have weaknesses we can capitalize on?" Blake asked.

"No," Nidhogg replied.

"Care to elaborate?" Blake pressed. "You managed to convince them to leave Fire Mountain."

"They wanted to go," one of the seers spoke up. "They have weaknesses, but you'd have to be another dragon to leverage them."

More wingbeats were followed by soft thuds as two

dragons, one red and the other blue, settled to earth on either side of the dais.

"Report," Dewi bugled.

If a dragon could look uncomfortable, this pair certainly did. The blue bugled, coughed, and bugled again before choking out, "They're, er, gone."

"You weren't absent very long," Dewi said. "Are you certain?"

"Aye, quite," the green replied. "No one has lived there for a very long while."

Before the dragons got lost pointing fingers and slinging accusations about who was to blame, I said, "These are your kinsmen who've gone astray. They have my daughter. I am requesting your assistance. We need it if we're to be successful retrieving her and Roya, her companion."

"We would indeed appreciate your cooperation," Blake cut in smoothly. "The Sidhe would be forever in your debt."

"Not what we've heard," Nidhogg grumbled. Smoke puffed from his flared nostrils.

"Aye, that daughter of yours has been naught but trouble," Dewi seconded. "The Sidhe may consider themselves well shut of her." She stopped for a moment. "Is that why you're here? Your army refused your orders?"

Blake walked down a few more steps. "Toss a truth net over me." He waited until one clanked into place and said, "My people are worried about Tiana. The army is mustering. We had both Sidhe and animals out hunting for our daughter before we discovered her whereabouts."

"Where did your information originate?" Dewi asked.

"The ley lines," I told her. "They will help, but their power is weak that deep in Hell."

Dewi turned to the seer nearest her. "What do you know about this?"

The seer bowed low before answering. "We did not know about the escape because it wasn't a question we asked any of our scrying tools."

"Never mind about who knew what." I sounded rude, but my concern for Tiana had escalated alarmingly. A couple of Leviathans was one thing; an entire herd of them quite another. This was shaping up to be a major magical power-grab using my daughter's fledgling enchantment as a lynchpin.

"We need to leave," Cailleach said.

"Agreed. Can we count on your aid?" Blake asked the dragons.

"What will you bring to the table?" Dewi countered.

"Arianrhod and Ceridwen. Possibly Gwydion and Bran," Blake replied. "I will ask Odin for his warriors, both living and dead."

"The unicorns will join us," I said. "As will any animal life forms we find in Hell."

"Their magic won't be effective in that portion of Hell," Nidhogg informed me.

We'd see about that. From what I knew, unicorn magic worked everywhere.

"We must be part of the upcoming battle," one of the seers told Nidhogg.

Trumpets, bugles, and a chorus of ayes rippled through

the chamber. Beyond storytelling, dragons lived for war, and there'd been precious few for a good long while.

The black dragon trumpeted loudly. "You know this, but missed the fact that all the Leviathans slipped beyond our grasp?"

The seer shrugged. His scales formed an iridescent wave pattern rippling along his torso. "We know what we know. It is not to be questioned."

Tidy response. I filed it away to use later.

Blake joined me and motioned to Cailleach who stood on my other side. "We are leaving. Our next stop is Asgard."

"If we decide to take part in this, we will join you there," Nidhogg said stiffly. He was being maneuvered into a corner and didn't care for it.

"Very well." Blake nodded curtly.

The familiar feel of his power swirled around me. The dragons could have held us, stopped our egress; they didn't.

"Was it worth all the time that took?" I mused out loud.

"Aye," Cailleach replied. "At least we know what we face."

"And I have a better idea what's in play," Blake said.

"How could they not know their kin gave them the slip?" I asked, understanding it was a rhetorical question.

"They're arrogant. Never occurred to them anyone wouldn't follow their edicts," Cailleach answered. "Particularly not their own blood."

"My bet is the Leviathans want revenge," Blake said. "Old wounds run deep. Dragons compounded their sins by first creating an inferior race and then banishing them so they wouldn't be faced with their shortcomings."

"Don't get mad, get even," I mumbled.

"Something like that," Blake agreed.

In far less time than our outbound journey had taken, we tumbled into a fairytale world with golden streets, golden buildings, and a castle perched at the top of a steep hill. I'd never been to Asgard before, and I turned in a circle taking everything in like a two-bit tourist at Buckingham Palace.

Odin's crows, Huginn and Muninn, winged toward us cawing up a storm. Still raising a racket, they settled on my shoulders. Odin galloped toward us astride his eight-legged steed, Sleipnir. The black horse nuzzled me when they drew near, getting horse drool all over my chest.

Odin leapt to the ground in a surprisingly graceful motion.

"The birds told me it was you. Welcome!"

He always looks the same. A mountain of a god, he stands slightly more than two meters. Almost as broad as he is tall, his naked neck, back, and shoulders were slabbed with muscle. A scraggly silver beard reached to mid-chest. Clinging like a second skin, leather breeks covered him from waist to ankle. His battle axe was strapped across his back with stout leather thongs.

His single gray eye was fixed on me. Actually on the part of my chest the horse had slobbered on. I stood tall beneath his scrutiny and reminded myself he could lech all he wanted. I was Blake's mate.

"Did you miss me?" He winked broadly.

I stroked the crows. "No, but they seem to have. Missed me, that is."

Sleipnir whinnied and dug his nose deeper into my cleavage. Regular chip off the old block, that one.

"Now that we are allies," Blake said, "I have come to request aid."

"What type of aid?" Odin wasn't staring at my breasts any longer.

"Our daughter has been taken by Leviathans," I said. "She's deep in Satan's realm."

Booming laughter rolled from him. "You need my army of the dead, eh? It could be arranged. What better place for them than Hell?"

"It's a lot of Leviathans," I added. "As in all of them."

Odin's gray brows inched up his forehead. "I thought they were with their dragon ancestors."

"So did the dragons until they took the time to actually look," Cailleach said dryly.

"You've been to Fire Mountain then?" Odin asked. When we all nodded, he said, "Didn't happen to see Nidhogg while you were there?"

"We did," Blake replied. "He will meet us here if the dragons deign to assist."

"Pfft." Odin freed his battle axe and chucked it into the dirt. "How could the dragons refuse? They're who lost track of their own."

The crows took up chittering again. Clearly, they held opinions about dragonkind.

Odin speared me with his one-eyed gaze. This time, he looked me in the eye. "Do you hold sway over them?"

I didn't have to reach to know he meant the dragons. Before I could answer, Cailleach said, "Aye and nay. She fascinates them, and some of the lesser dragons do her bidding. The elders wanted to hold onto her. It's possible they view her as a threat to their autonomy."

"Yet they allowed her to depart." Odin stated the obvious.

"They didn't have much choice without alienating the Sidhe," Blake explained.

A rustle from behind made me swing my head around in time to see Hel and her serpents emerge from an opening in the ground that closed once they passed through. I held out a hand. "Well met, sister."

The cobras glided my way, wrapping around my lower body. Hel grasped my hand. Tall and slender with long dark hair, she'd been banished to Niflheim because half her body was nothing but bones. According to legend, Odin found the sight of her so disturbing, he assigned her the job of tending the dead.

"Well met, indeed," she purred and patted one of the cobra's heads.

"Excellent timing," Odin boomed. "Another war awaits us."

"Really?" A dark brow arched on the flesh side of her face. "With whom?"

"Leviathans."

"Aren't they protected by the Fire Mountain dragons?"

I let go of her hand and sketched out what she needed to know.

"I see," she said, thoughtfully.

"No sign of Nidhogg." Odin shielded his eye with a hand

and scanned the skies as if it would bring the miscreant Norse dragon to heel.

"Not yet," Blake agreed. "We're returning to Underhill. I'll raise Arianrhod to see how she did with the Celts."

"I'll figure out where the unicorns are," I murmured, "even though Nidhogg doesn't believe their power will extend that far into Hell."

"What's your timeframe?" Odin was all business, so I assumed we could count on his support.

"As soon as possible," Blake said. "I'd like to launch not later than tomorrow night."

"Are we teleporting or battling our way through Hell?" Odin asked.

"Depends if the dragons sign on," Blake answered. "If they do, I'm guessing they have ways of latching onto where their blood resides. It would save a lot of warriors if we didn't have to engage at every gateway."

I've been in Hell, but not the lower regions. From Blake's words, I gathered demons were posted at each level to discourage nonessential visitors. "When I healed the ley lines," I said slowly, "I was somewhere in Hell, but they told me they wouldn't be much help where Tiana is."

"When I found you, it was between the first and second levels," Blake informed me.

Whoa. Long way from there to the Ninth Gate. No wonder the lines had sounded unsure about how far their power would stretch.

"Charon and I are old acquaintances," I said. "He might know secret ways deeper into Hell. If he wouldn't have helped me, I'd have had a much harder time locating the lines."

"Where will we meet?" Odin asked.

I glanced at Blake. Battle strategy isn't one of my fortes. I've worked alone most of my long life.

"How about back here?" Blake suggested. "Asgard holds its own magic. We will be moving large numbers. Unless we break into groups like we did during the vampire confrontation, we'll need a magical assist getting into position."

"If we start here, I lead," Odin said flatly.

Too late, I remembered his and Blake's last go round vying for the top dog spot.

Blake faced off in front of him. "Co-leaders. It's my daughter who's in trouble."

"I have more battle experience."

"Doubt it," Blake shot back.

"For Danu's sake, stop it," I shouted. "If the fucking dragons show up, they'll want to run the show."

"Ain't that the truth," Cailleach muttered *sotto voce*.

"Co leaders." Odin stuck out a beefy hand. Blake shook it.

Before I could bid Hel farewell, a journey spell boiled around me. The crows and serpents untangled themselves in a hurry. Magical creatures understand spells, and none of them wanted a free ride to wherever we were going.

I smelled Underhill before it took shape around us.

"I'll hunt down the Celts," Cailleach said.

"I'm going to check in with Breanne and the Sidhe army," Blake said and turned to me. "I have a task for you if you're up for it."

"What?" I'd been planning to read up on Hell, but everyone else held the knowledge I lacked.

"I had no idea you knew Charon. Could you find him? Perhaps he'd help much the same way he did with the ley lines."

I nodded. "I can try. He wasn't exactly delighted to see me since I was in the no-man's land that's barred to the living."

"Trying works for me." Blake turned away.

Cailleach was already gone. I cobbled a quick spell together and aimed for the River Styxx. My last trip, I'd been intent on the ley lines and had crossed a forbidden boundary. I'd do my best to locate him on the proper side.

Might work. Or might not. I was painfully aware of time getting away from us. Blake had pegged tomorrow night to launch our rescue effort. Would it be too late? If Tiana was dead, surely I'd know. She's as immortal as I am, yet some paths are worse than being dead.

I put a plug in my dark thoughts. I had to believe we'd get her back. She'd be changed. No one could live through what she was probably suffering and not have it scar them. But I'd give anything to feel her arms around me again. To see the joy a group of animals gave her.

My spell spit me out on the banks of the River Styxx. It was running higher than usual, but the boat was in its usual spot. Boded well that Charon wasn't ferrying souls across the abyss.

Cerebrus ran to me baying a greeting. Three tongues licked effusively. One tail wagged. I petted him, soaking up love and hope.

"Back again so soon?" Charon's deep voice preceded his form. Garbed in homespun gray robes the same color as his hound, he had a white beard that reached the ground, empty eye sockets, and gnarled fingers with many silver rings. In an odd way, he reminded me of Hel.

"'Fraid so."

He opened his arms; I walked into them. It was tough not to cry, but I held myself together as the story about Tiana's capture spilled from me. I ended with, "You helped me find the ley lines. Can you help me find my daughter?"

Charon stroked hair back from my face and held me. "I heard rumors, yet had no idea they were about your daughter."

"Can you help?"

"Have you asked the dragons? They can locate their kinsmen."

I nodded. "Yeah. They're thinking about it."

"Oh, so that's how it is." He released me and blew out a tired-sounding breath. Next, he touched my eyelids. My eyes closed; images flooded my mind. From one level of Hell to the next until no more pictures came.

"Remember the order," he cautioned.

"But it's impossible. Not the remembering, but how will we make it through all those barriers?"

"Not impossible, child, but also far from simple. You cannot take the unicorns."

"Why not? And how did you know I was planning to?"

"How else? I saw it in your mind. They cannot survive that deep in Hell. Much like the ley lines, their power degrades beyond the third or fourth gate."

Cerebrus rubbed one of his heads against my thigh.

Charon dropped a hand on my shoulder. "You must leave now. I do not have a good feeling about any of this. The sooner you retrieve your daughter, the better chance she'll..."

Fear speared me; my gut wouldn't have hurt worse if I'd been stabbed. "She'll what?"

He tightened his grip. "Not be so changed you no longer recognize her. Time among Leviathans does that to anyone. They selected her for a reason. It wasn't random."

"We figured it was a way to get to me and the ley lines."

"Might be part of it, but why not just grab you instead? Wouldn't have cost them that much more."

"Got it." My chest was so tight I could barely breathe, but I managed to thank the boatman before my next spell took me back to Underhill. We couldn't wait until tomorrow. We had to leave as soon as we amassed a force that had a chance of defeating the bastards who'd stolen my daughter.

We need the dragons...

We'll do this with or without them, I answered myself.

Underhill bloomed around me; I took off at a run in search of Blake.

CHAPTER 14
TIANA

The monster who'd had hold of me lunged, intent on reestablishing his power position. It taught me I was quicker and more maneuverable than him—and all the rest of them too.

All the rest of them.

My eyes had adapted to the unnatural brilliance from the many fires. The cavern was enormous. Leviathans filled it as far as I could see. My pivot-and-evade maneuvers might work against one—or maybe two—of them, but a wall of reptilian flesh slithered toward me.

I could deflect them for a while. Eventually, they'd crush me. I stared at the nearest ones and somersaulted out of their path only to end up uncomfortably close to three more.

Suddenly, it hit me. They had wings, but their appendages were far too small to support them. Probably part of their dragon heritage, but useless.

I timed my next move carefully. By now, the entire room

had mobilized against me, growing ever closer amid grunts and hissing snarls. Ash, smoke, and steam added to the cavern's already unbearable heat.

Hop. Pivot. Leap. My wings snapped out, and I was airborne and flapping desperately to gain altitude. The domed top of the cavern was far above me, well beyond the Leviathans' reach. The higher I went, the more oppressive the heat grew until I was panting. Dragging air into my struggling lungs was tough since each breath seared delicate tissue and made the next one that much harder.

Every last drop of moisture fled from my body, no more sweat left. It was dangerous, but I couldn't remember why.

Beneath me, chaos erupted. The creatures reached as far as they could, balanced on haunches, forelegs extended.

"Land immediately, or things will not go well for you," someone bellowed.

Aho! So they didn't require telepathy after all.

I scribed circles high above the throng, drawing on magic like a madwoman. This was my only chance, but it was precarious. I'd run out of energy and magic long before the crowd grew bored and left. Heat and fear are a shitty combination. My mind grew sluggish.

Pull it together, a voice that sounded suspiciously like Breanne's shouted.

I blinked stupidly, expecting to see her flying alongside me. No such luck. My addled brain was playing tricks on me. I flew higher searching for a place I could stop and rest. Nothing caught my eye.

Did I dare try to teleport out of this mess?

If I did, it would mean leaving Roya to her fate. I tried

telling myself Mother and Father would show up soon with the Sidhe army, but I couldn't square abandoning my friend. I could probably teleport back to her. Maybe. The place we'd been sequestered was surrounded by a barrier.

If I got lucky and broke through it, the bastards below would just find me again.

But if I break through, it means I can take Roya and leave...

Yeah, and if I don't I'll end up sprawled in the middle of those ravening beasts.

Any resemblance to rationality had departed once I took to the air. Leviathans bellowed, trumpeted, and cursed me roundly. My affinity for the animal world didn't extend to them.

Or did it?

Nothing ventured, nothing gained. "Stop that this minute," I shouted in an epic imitation of Kirwan. No one broke stride or even looked up. Cheers exploded, confusing me. None of the Leviathans had paid the slightest heed to my order. What the hell was there to cheer about?

I scanned the ground. Endless coils stretched to infinity. Unlike dragons with their myriad colors, all of these fuckers were gray. My shoulders ached, the muscles on fire. I'd never flown this long before. A dark blob detached itself from the throng, spread coal-black wings, and headed straight toward me.

Fuckity fuck.

Not a Leviathan, but some other Hell-spawned atrocity. As it closed on me, I saw dark hair, fiery eyes, and a body that could have belonged to one of the gods. Hell, for all I knew the thing was a god.

Batting for the other side.

He was unspeakably gorgeous. Pale skin stretched over arched cheekbones. Gleaming teeth were set in a square jaw. He opened his arms invitingly. "Come to me, little one. You must be exhausted."

I started to nod but caught myself. Ensorcellment hung in the air around him, almost visible if I looked through my third eye. Crap. Why hadn't I paid closer attention when Kirwan tried to teach me about all the evils in the world?

"Friends wait below," he went on in silken tones. "They would set you above them as their queen."

"Ha. Funny way to treat me, then," I rasped from a throat so dry it could have been lined with sandpaper.

"Give them a chance." He flew closer, arms still extended.

Damn it. I wanted to fly into them and let him hold me. Sensations I'd never known existed washed through me. Longing with a special ache in my nipples and groin. What was happening?

"That's it," he crooned. "Come to me, little one. I'll take care of you."

Far below, the crowd of Leviathans had grown silent. Many eyes were trained on us as if our aerial ballet was a spectator sport.

I had to keep my eyes open to see where I was flying, but I tore my gaze from the dark angel—or whatever he was— luring me to my doom. Not staring into those bottomless red eyes helped a little. My breath came in little spurting pants. My shoulders had turned into unimaginable agony.

I flew on.

"I am Raphael," my airborne companion said. "One of three archangels."

So we were on a first-name basis, eh. Avoiding his gaze, I stared at his black wings. Larger than mine, they cleaved the air effortlessly. I envied him that.

"Let me help," he repeated.

An infusion of cooler air surrounded me. Something flowed into my magical center, augmenting my flagging energy. Shame on me, but I sucked it in brazenly, and then returned to the well for more.

Did this work like the Leviathan drinking my blood? If I accepted gifts, was I then beholden to Raphael? At least the squirmy pleasurable sensations had retreated. Maybe he'd figured out I was only twelve.

Who am I kidding? He doesn't give a fuck. He wants something from me, but he'd prefer me to be a willing participant, or he'd have snatched me out of the air.

The realization dug deep. He was toying with me. He had all the time in the world. We both knew I'd run out of steam and fall into the sea of open jaws waiting below.

"I can save you from them," rustled through my mind. *"They're primitive, savages. Come with me. I shall make you my queen."*

"I'm already a queen," I mumbled.

"Nay. The Sidhe will forget about you, but I never will. Besides, they don't require a regent."

"But first you said I'd be their"—I pointed below—"queen."

"Did I now?"

I did my damnedest to kickstart my fuzzy brain into

some semblance of order. None of this was adding up. Presumably, Raphael had shown up because the Leviathans called him into action. He had the wings they lacked. Yet he was kicking them to the curb.

Or was he? Talk is cheap.

Were the beasts roaming below as dumb as they looked? Dragons were supposed to be smart. For the millionth time, I wished I'd paid better attention to Kirwan's lessons. He'd tried to teach me about dragons and sea serpents and Leviathans. Roya knew far more about them than me.

Raphael's name struck a distant chord, but I couldn't pigeonhole it, either. Every single time I lifted my shoulders, pain shot through my whole upper back. Sheer will kept me in the air. Were it not for the infusion of power and cooler air floating around me, I'd have faltered and fallen.

"See? I'm helping you." He beckoned with both hands. "Come to me. It won't be all that bad. I'll even let you tell your parents goodbye."

"They're coming," I choked out.

He nodded, dark hair floating around his angelic face. "Aye, that they are. But not for a while, and with too small a force to make much difference. You don't want to place them in danger. I can fix everything."

"How?" I croaked and kicked myself. He was engaging me in dialogue, a slippery slope for me. It placed us on the same side, forging a relationship when what I should be doing was fighting back.

How? A bitter inner voice demanded, followed by, *with what?*

"I will teach you," Raphael went on. "You hold untapped

strengths that have yet to be released. You will grow into incredible power. I shall be the one standing by your side. We could rule together."

"Rule what?" I choked out.

A slight whisper of the pleasurable sensations he'd bombarded me with earlier caressed me.

I shuddered. "Stop that."

"As you wish." He inclined his head. "You are young. Someday, you will appreciate what a man has to offer."

Breath stuttered from my tired lungs. At least he wasn't intent on raping me. I'd read stories about unfortunate girls, stories in the forbidden section of the Sidhe library. I'd had to leverage surreptitious power to access those particular books and scrolls.

"I told you I'd never hurt you." Raphael sounded wounded.

"Stay out of my mind."

He shrugged. "Not until you acquiesce." Pointing downward, he said, "No way out, little one. Except with me."

Even if everything else that had crossed his lips were lies, his last statement rang with an unfortunate truth. An idea gripped me. Hoping it worked out better than my leap into the air one had, I gently probed to find where he'd linked with my thoughts.

When I found the threads, I tracked them back to his mind, intent on trolling for better options.

And fell headlong into a swirling plethora of memories. A victorious whoop from him told me I'd waltzed right into a trap he'd set. When I tried to back out—and couldn't—I dove in deeper.

I couldn't undo my mistake, but if I was quick maybe I'd profit from it yet. I swam through millennia of memories. He was old, unbelievably old. I'd thought the Sidhe went back a long way, but our history is nothing compared with his.

He was trying to talk with me; I tuned him out determined to discover something that might give me an edge. His arms were around me now; I didn't fight him. No longer flying was an unbelievable relief.

The Leviathans were still bellowing. And then their voices faded.

Raphael had moved us somewhere else. I stopped trolling through his history long enough to take in a well-appointed sitting room with a marble hearth and thick rugs.

"Go ahead, little one. Look to your heart's content," he urged.

I'd expected him to fight me. Having his permission iced my bones. What happened once I reached the end of those thousands and thousands of years? Would I be inextricably bound to him?

"You already are, darling."

I tried to disengage again, and failed. Whenever I drew back, I became disoriented. My life was part of his now. It always had been, always would be. When I tried to dredge up visions of Underhill, of Mother and Father, they were fuzzy and insubstantial.

Finally, I gave up and started asking questions. "What battle was that one?"

"When the dragons challenged the Celts."

I shook my head. "Never heard about it."

"You wouldn't have. It predates Sidhe lore."

"Who is she?" I stared at a lissome redhead standing in front of piles of rubble holding a golden scepter.

"Pele."

"The fire goddess?"

"The same."

Unlike Kirwan, Raphael had infinite patience for my questions. At some point, he left and returned with a sparkling mead and sweetmeats. I continued my exploration even with him gone.

Did it mean the linkage he'd alluded to was so solidly constructed no one could break it? I tried to gin up Mother's face and couldn't recall quite what she looked like other than her hair was red like mine.

I broke off my trip through Raphael's long life to say, "I'm never going back, am I?"

He sat in a black leather easy chair, legs sprawled on a hassock. For the first time, I noticed he wore buff-colored trousers, lace-up boots, and a leather jerkin over everything.

"What do you think?" he countered.

"I'm stuck here."

The pleasant expression on his face shattered. On his feet so fast I couldn't follow his movements, he crossed to where I sat and slapped me hard.

"'Tis an honor I have extended to you, one never tendered to another mage."

The side of my face smarted. I refused to rub it. Struggling to my feet, I faced him. "You will not—"

Another slap; this one harder.

He leaned close. "You are no longer a Sidhe princess. You

belong to me. When you walked into my mind, you sealed our affiliation. There is no going back."

His hand snaked out, grabbed my shoulder, and shook me. "I offer you limitless power. In return, I demand absolute obedience and loyalty. Do we understand one another?"

The superhighway into his thoughts shut off abruptly. "I shall return in a bit. You will have an answer for me."

"About?" I've had plenty of practice being insolent, but I didn't want him to hit me again.

"I was quite clear. Either you stand with me, or I toss you back to the Leviathans."

One moment he stood before me; the next he was gone.

I sank to the floor and wrapped my arms around my knees. For the hell of it, I tested my magic. It was weak and bounced back to slap me when I tried a teleport spell.

I'd been a fool to think he'd allow me to leave.

I was also dead out of choices. I had been from the moment the monsters dragged me from Roya's side.

Roya.

Was she still alive? Had they taken their ire against me out on her? I said a small prayer to Danu, asking for grace. I'm not the praying type, but I kept at it.

Not the anything type, actually.

And now I was slated to marry evil. Eh, he hadn't said crap about a marriage. He'd take me when he was good and ready, no vows needed.

I slammed a fist down on the rug. There had to be a way out of this. I refused to concede defeat. When Rafael returned, I'd pretend to be grateful to see him. Young as I was, I knew how egotistical men were and what fools they could be where anything female was concerned.

And then I took care to shield my thoughts. He'd read them as easily as an open scroll.

"That's it," I mumbled out loud. "Childhood is officially over."

For some reason, the words amused me. So did all my promises to mend my lackluster ways. I'd never have an opportunity now. Raphael had said I'd get a chance to say goodbye to my parents, but I didn't believe him.

I mowed through the rest of the sweetmeats and drank the last of the mead. No reason to starve. I needed fuel to figure this out. When I felt stronger, I'd try my magic once more. If I could just get to Roya, I could give her messages for the parents I barely remembered.

"Eh, why bother?" a voice I didn't recognize cut in.

My eyes snapped open. Had a new side of me cropped up? No one else was close enough to talk with me.

Or were they?

Focusing on my ward, I wrapped it even more snugly around my mind. No matter what happened, I'd make the best of things. Not today, and not tomorrow, but sometime, my jailers would relax. They had to. If I were patient—not one of my better habits—I'd figure this out.

"Things are decent here," the same voice drawled.

It gave me the creeps. Was I changing even as I sat here? I'd broken a bunch of rules. Leviathans had drunk my blood. I'd eaten food without considering what it might have been laced with. I'd traipsed through Raphael's mind.

Before despair trapped me in inertia, I got back to my

feet and began a systematic exploration of the room. It diverted me, gave me a task, and passed the time in one fell swoop.

Meanwhile, the new voice kept on nattering. None of my other inner voices said boo. Ignoring everything but my self-appointed task, I started with the desk in the corner. Littered with scrolls, it would provide hours of reading.

Heedless of consequences, I unrolled the top one, read the first few lines, and understood it was an ancient grimoire. I tried to roll it back up, but it stabbed my fingers. The scroll danced to life around me as my blood wetted the archaic vellum.

Ghouls, soul-suckers, demons, and things I had no names for entered the room welcoming me into the fold. The girl I'd been was dying, edged out by evil.

Nothing I could do would bring her back. I should care. I tried marshaling my resources—whatever was left of them —to fight the transformation.

My efforts were laughable, mostly because all I felt was numb. My shoulders still ached from all my time in the air. When I glanced at a wing, I cringed. No longer a pretty green, it was shading to black.

Was the rest of me changing too?

I knocked over the chair in my haste to run to an ornamental mirror hung over the marble hearth. I had to stand on tiptoe to see myself.

Nothing of the child I'd been remained. My hair was still red, my eyes still green, but my face had altered to planes and angles. My chin jutted from a clenched lower jaw. The net effect was I looked all grown up but not in a pretty way. My features had turned harsh, foreboding.

Doubling up a fist, I slammed it into the mirror. The surface shimmered before settling. When it did, ghouls ringed my reflection. I hadn't felt them draw near.

"You're home," one crowed and stroked my arm with spectral fingers.

"We've waited long for you," another growled.

"Read this." A red-scaled demon waved a scroll over his horned head.

Not likely. If it was anything like the last scroll, all I had to do was lay eyes on it, and it would go into attack mode.

Walking a balance beam over a fiery pit would have been simpler. I trudged back to a chair, avoiding the desk. When the demon dropped the scroll into my lap, I pushed it to one side.

"Leave me to rest," I ordered, not expecting anything.

The unearthly collection of monsters faded from view. I blinked at where they'd stood. Had they ever been real?

Didn't matter. My eyes shut. I'd grab rest where I could. Raphael would be back expecting an answer, and I had no idea what to tell him. The specter of ruling by his side was attractive.

Too attractive.

If I told him yes, it would be the death knell for everything I'd held dear.

Yeah, and if I tell him no, I'm done for.

Trapped between two unpleasant options, I blocked out everything and sought relief in sleep. Didn't work very well. My mind was too busy running like a rat trapped in a maze. I was still sitting in the same chair when a door I hadn't noticed swung open.

Rafael strode through wearing his "nice" face. The one that had tricked me into believing he cared what happened to me. I didn't get up, mostly to see if he'd rebuke me for insolence.

"Before I left, I posed a question. Do you have an answer?" He arched a dark brow.

"Yeah, I believe I do." I was buying time. Sooner or later, I'd have to spit something out. If I told him yes, the sliver of me that remained would be lost forever. If I told him no, the net result would be the same.

Better to live, no matter how shitty the circumstances.

Slowly, I pushed to my feet and faced my nemesis.

The enemy who'd run ragged over me without a second thought. He needed me for something, or I'd already have hit the slag heap.

"My answer is yes, but with conditions."

"You're scarcely in a position to bargain," he noted wryly.

"Oh, but I believe I am." My throat was dry, breath coming quickly. I'd tossed down a gauntlet. Would I have the nerve to stand my ground?

The ghouls, soul-suckers, and demons formed a group off to one side, their attention glued on me. They were waiting for something. Would Raphael toss me their way as a prize piece of meat if I didn't go along with his wishes?

Fear rode me like a worn-out nag, but I couldn't give in. Not now, and never to him.

CHAPTER 15
BLAKE

I was putting the finishing touches on our troop deployment when Abria pitched into the council chamber at a dead run. One look at her white face brought me to my feet. When she reached me, I swept her into my arms.

"What's wrong? Did you not find Charon?"

"Oh I found him, all right." Her voice was muffled in the hollow between my neck and shoulder. "He showed me all the barriers we must cross."

A series of images spilled through my mind. The front ones looked familiar, the later ones not so much. My assessment about losing half the Sidhe army wasn't far off base.

"We need the dragons," Abria said. "And the Celts."

"We have Odin and his merry band," I reminded her.

"They won't be enough. We can't involve the unicorns. Charon said their magic doesn't work that deep in Hell."

Nidhogg had intimated much the same. I let go of her

and tried to lighten the mood. "What we have might be enough. Since when did you become a seer?"

"I trust Charon. According to him, we must move now. We cannot afford to wait even until tomorrow."

I angled my head. "Did he say why?"

She nodded slowly. "Tiana may well already be lost to us. Each passing hour lessens the chances of successfully retrieving her."

I'd already guessed as much. No one traffics with evil without being touched by its slime.

"Abria. Look at me."

She did, and I went on. "We must maximize our chances of success. Rushing forward headlong won't help Tiana—or us. Also, I haven't given up on the dragons. They're a responsible crew. I can't see them brushing off such an egregious act by their blood kin."

Abria frowned. "I still think we should position ourselves in Asgard. We're leaving from there, right?"

"Aye. We can do that. I've been waiting for Cailleach."

Abria slapped her forehead with one palm. "Fuck. I forgot about her going to rustle up the Celts."

"Valuable allies—if they get off their asses and decide we're worthy of their time."

"But this whole mess is Arianrhod's fault," Abria protested. "If she'd kept an eye on Tiana, like she was supposed to—"

"Neither here nor there," I broke in. "If Tiana hadn't been such a pain in the butt, we'd never have farmed her out to Caer Sidi."

Breanne bustled into the room, axe fastened across her broad back. "The troops are ready to depart, Regent."

"Good. Teleport to Asgard. Wait for me there."

"For how long."

I felt like snapping, *forever if need be.* Instead, I said, "I'm waiting on Cailleach and hopefully a few Celts."

"Don't tarry too long," Breanne cautioned in a repeat of Abria's we-need-to-leave-now message.

"I won't."

She clapped a fist over her heart and bowed. I repeated the gesture, warlord to chief general.

Once she was gone, I turned to Abria. "Change into sturdier clothes, something that will deflect heat. Get something to eat."

She shook her head. "I'm not leaving your side. What if Cailleach returns? I might miss something, and—"

"I'll call you. Feed your magic. It needs to be in tip-top shape."

Abria turned and hurried from the council chamber. It was unlike her not to argue, which told me how desperate she was.

Regardless, something I'd said got through, even if it had been harsher than I'd intended. I was frantic about Tiana, but not so rattled I'd willingly make mistakes. If the dragons saw their way clear to provide journey spells to reach their kinsmen, it would make a huge difference. We'd bypass battles at each of Hell's gates.

Arriving with our full force intact could make the difference between success and... I stumbled over the word *failure,* loathe to even think it.

Tiana was plucky. If anyone was equipped to come through this, it was her.

She's only a child, and a spoiled one at that. How gutsy could she be?

I shushed my thoughts and focused on positive outcomes. The trick to anything magical is envisioning what you want to have happen. Summoning a vision of my daughter, I told her she was strong beyond measure, that she'd muscle through this.

It was silly. She couldn't hear me, not over the distance separating us, but it made me feel better.

No reason to hang around the council chamber. Underhill would inform me about any visitors. Deciding to take my own advice, I loped to the rooms Abria, Tiana, and I share. Abria was tugging clothes over her damp body. The steamy air told me she'd rinsed off.

"Good idea," I mumbled and stripped out of my garments.

The hot water helped me think. Back in our sleeping chamber with a towel wrapped around my waist, I said, "Thank you."

"For what?" Abria was winding her long hair into braids and tucking them under the collar of a heavy denim jacket. Her voice sounded dull, dead.

"Not fighting me on this."

She rounded on me, her green eyes pinched with agony. "What if she dies? What if we're too late?"

"Do. Not. Entertain. Such. Thoughts." I anchored each word with a calming spell.

"You're right, of course. But I'm scared for her. She's all bluster and no substance."

I put my arms around my mate and held on tight for a long moment before letting go and dredging clothes from a nearby armoire.

"Give her credit," I suggested. "She's not as tough as she'd like everyone to believe, but she's far from a pushover."

"She's rude to us and the Sidhe, but she's never had to deal with evil before." Abria's eyes shone with tears.

"Don't give up." My words were soft. "This isn't over. Until it is, we will maintain hope." I paused for a moment before adding, "You were resourceful at her age."

"Nah, I was closer to twenty."

"Not that much difference," I insisted.

I was dressed and shoving my feet into heavy boots when a glowing portal formed. Abria had been slumped against a wall. She shot upright, hands raised and power crackling between her fingertips.

"Stand down," I told her. "They're Celts."

She dropped her arms to her sides, muttering, "Fuck. I really am losing it."

I'd expected Arianrhod, and I wasn't disappointed. With her were Ceridwen, Gwydion, and Bran. I hadn't seen the men for at least 500 years. After bowing low, I extended a hand. Both gods shook it.

"Thank you for coming," Abria said.

Gwydion twisted to face her. "Mmph. Haven't seen you since you rejected our hospitality."

He's the Celts' warrior magician. Blond hair was braided

tight against his skull in a Celtic knot pattern. Blue eyes held a somber note. His robe matched his eyes; it was double sashed in white silk and a leather belt riddled with pouches that presumably held magical accoutrements. Leather sandals covered his feet.

I was afraid Abria would rise to the bait and tell him his hospitality had been sorely lacking. Instead, she smiled and extended her hand. "It's been too long."

After a pause, he touched her hand, but didn't shake it.

Bran ambled forward. Red hair was cropped short; his dark eyes probably didn't miss much. Specially made armor swathed his bulk. A broadsword was lashed to his back. Unlike Gwydion, no greetings flowed from him. Instead, he was all business.

"Do you hold knowledge beyond what Arianrhod has relayed?" he asked in a deep voice.

"Perhaps, since I have no idea what Cailleach told you. Odin stands with us. We will assemble our forces in Asgard."

"Charon showed me pictures of the various gates in Hell," Abria offered.

"Pfft." Bran waved a hand. "Already know about them."

"Any further word from the dragons?" Cailleach asked.

"Nope," Abria said, and then added, "Would any of you care for nourishment? There's not much time, but—"

"There is no time, child," Ceridwen snarled. Her cauldron plunked down beside her to emphasize her words.

I eyed it and asked, "Any word from that quarter?"

"Nothing new except we must hurry," she responded.

Same message from three different sources. Odd numbers hold a power all their own. "The Sidhe army is already in Asgard. Shall we join them?" I glanced at the group.

"Depends," Gwydion said. "Who is leading the troops?"

"Odin and I will be splitting that responsibility, but there is always room for one more," I told him.

The warrior magician tilted his chin. "I will be in charge."

Okay, then.

"Fine by me," I said, "but I can't speak for Odin."

"Or the dragons if they happen to show up," Abria tossed out.

Celtic power thickened in the room. It's not unlike Sidhe enchantment in that it smells of the natural world. In this instance, wildflowers mingled with rain-wet greenery. With no transition time, we walked into the center of Asgard's square.

Sidhe and Norse warriors milled about. Valkyries swooped overhead. No dragons.

Not yet, I told myself, refusing to give up.

Odin galloped toward us on Sleipnir, skidding to a halt in front of the Celtic contingent. "Gone slumming?" he inquired blandly.

"Something like that," Bran shot back.

Odin turned to me. "I did not agree with including them."

Oh-oh. Diplomacy time.

"You knew Arianrhod and Ceridwen would be part of our group," I reminded him. "What's a couple more. Not as if we don't need all the help we can get."

"If they'd actually help," Odin said loud enough for everyone to hear.

Gwydion chose that moment to step forward. "I lead our charge, or I leave."

Odin jumped down from Sleipnir and dusted his hands together before making shooing motions with them. "That was easy. Nice to see you. Bye."

I inserted my body between them. "Let's not be hasty," I told Odin.

"I laid out my terms," Gwydion said.

Odin skewered me with his one gray eye. "And you agreed with letting him lead the Sidhe? I'm shocked, Elwyn."

"It was the only way to secure his assistance," I said stiffly. "Can we get moving? How bad will it be to cede control for a single battle?"

"My people will never accept him," Odin said flatly.

As if she'd been listening, a Valkyrie swooped past, brushing a wing against Gwydion's ear. He shook a fist her way; she bared her teeth and hissed.

I wanted to shake sense into everyone. Their spawn wasn't missing. No skin off their asses if they stood and argued all day long about who would do what.

Abria shot me a desperate look. I didn't require words to interpret it. We needed to be gone yesterday, but we required a cohesive force. I gathered my thoughts and opened my mouth prepared to make a pitch for unity—just this once. After we returned, everyone could retreat to their corner of the sandbox and throw rocks at each other.

In a private quadrant of my mind, I didn't blame Odin.

The Celts had always been arrogant and close to impossible to work with.

Of course, he had too.

Takes one to know one...

I took my time before I spoke to ensure I wouldn't step too hard on anyone's precious ego. Guess I took too long because Abria shouted, "I can't believe all of you. My daughter is missing, and all you can do is—"

A crash from above was followed by the unmistakable beat of dragon wings. I craned my neck and stared skyward. Would it only be one? Or had Nidhogg talked others into joining him.

More noise suggested other dragons had broken through the barrier wrapped around the Nine Worlds. My nails dug into my fisted hands; I kept my gaze trained on the skies.

Nidhogg's black bulk heaved into view, followed by Dewi's unmistakable red form. Two might be enough to see us safely through Hell. I flexed my fingers and dragged air into my lungs.

Between one breath and the next, a string of dragons flew across the sky. Nidhogg plopped to the ground in front of Odin. The other five dragons landed nearby.

"Where have you been?" Odin stared up at the Norse dragon.

"Busy."

"Mmph. Wouldn't hurt if you stopped by occasionally."

Steam puffed from black jaws and wafted around Odin in a dragon peace offering. "I'm here now. As are some of my people. This is what we shall do to rectify the Leviathans' unfortunate act."

Gwydion stomped next to Odin. "I am in charge here. All decisions run through me."

The other dragons bugled what might have been laughter. Nidhogg stared at the Celt out of whirling eyes. "You overstep yourself."

"Eh. This was a bad idea. I'm leaving."

Abria ran to him. "Please. We need you."

He barely glanced at her. "Then allow me to do what I do best."

"Your opinion," Nidhogg trumpeted. "Do you know the way to the Leviathans' lair?" When Gwydion didn't answer, the dragon went on, "Do you understand how to defeat the Ninth Gate without engaging in a pitched battle?"

The Celts have many unsavory traits but lying isn't among them. Gwydion's silence spoke volumes. Surely, he understood how unprepared he was to lead our mission.

In the interest of setting a solid example, I said, "The Sidhe willingly accept direction from dragonkind."

"As do my troops," Odin said as he swung onto Nidhogg's broad back at the junction where his shoulders joined it.

Sleipnir neighed furiously and ran at the dragon. Odin held up a hand; it stopped the horse in his tracks. After a tense moment, Sleipnir turned and trotted away.

Gwydion walked to Dewi and vaulted into position.

Fire streamed from her jaws. "I did not give you permission to ride me."

"You are our dragon. I don't require permission."

The fire turned to a stream of ashy smoke, but Dewi didn't order him down. What she did do was raise her voice and thunder. "None of the other dragons will bear riders. Do I make myself clear?"

"Abundantly." I bowed.

"I will open a travel channel large enough to accommodate us all," Nidhogg said. "It is different from the ones you normally use. There will be little to no air, so plan wisely. The transit will take time, yet not enough to render you unconscious."

"Where will we emerge?" Gwydion asked.

"On the far side of the Ninth Gate, In position to deal with the Leviathans."

"Do you have a plan for them?" Ceridwen asked.

The black dragon nodded. Smoke plumed from his nostrils. The goddess stared at him, but he didn't offer any more details.

"Prepare yourselves," Nidhogg bellowed. "We leave in ten, nine, eight, seven..."

I wrapped an arm around Abria and used magic to form a bubble around us that trapped enough air to last for a while.

"No one said anything about finding Tiana, only about punishing the Leviathans," she murmured.

I switched to mind speech. *"'Tis a gift the dragons are here and helping us."* Nidhogg hadn't said anything about how we'd get back. Absent dragon help, we'd have to fight our way through all the levels of Hell the same way we'd have had to fight our way in.

At least our troops would be up to the task and not sorely depleted. Still, we'd sustain significant losses.

Focus on now. We're not even there yet, a wise inner voice counseled.

Tension radiated from Abria. I didn't voice my latest concern about our return journey. We'd take this one step at a time. We wouldn't be involved in whatever transpired between the Leviathans and their dragon overlords. It would free us to hunt for Tiana.

Nidhogg's countdown finished. Superheated air surrounded us smelling of sulfur and brimstone. Demon scents, but also the same smells I'd encountered in Fire Mountain.

An undulating tunnel formed. Nidhogg marched into it with Odin on his back. Dewi and Gwydion followed. And then the other Celts and Cailleach. Odin's contingent was swallowed by the dragon's spell. I shooed my army through next. Before I ducked inside, I called to one of the remaining dragons, "Are you coming?"

"Aye, Regent. We were instructed to go last to maintain the integrity of Nidhogg's casting."

It made sense. Not much I could to if the rear quadrant of the spell ran out of magic or chose to collapse.

With my arm still firmly around Abria, we entered the passageway. Magic pressed down on us from all sides. I took care to guard our precious oxygen supply. Nidhogg had said this wouldn't take long, but time runs differently in dragon circles.

Shudders ran through Abria's body where it pressed against mine.

"Are you all right?" I asked.

"Not even close. You?"

"Every minute draws us nearer to Tiana," I reminded her before I stopped talking. We needed to conserve the air in our bubble.

Waiting is hard, but this particular journey was the most difficult one in my life. We were sucking fumes before we stumbled out into unimaginable heat and brilliance that seared my retinas.

It took a moment to understand no one was engaged in a battle. The dragons that had been behind me weren't there any longer.

Breanne made her way to me. "There you are. Orders, Regent."

"Let me figure out what's going on. Where did the dragons go?"

She shrugged broad shoulders. "Haven't seen them since we walked out of their spell."

Damn it. I'd been afraid they'd forget we needed assistance returning.

Nidhogg's bulk pushed toward us. When he was close, he said, "Sidhe. I have spoken with my wayward kin. They informed me they did kidnap both your daughter and another mage."

"Aye, Roya," I said.

He made a snorting noise. "She's on her way to meet you."

"Where is Tiana?" Abria asked in a strangled tone.

Nidhogg shrugged amid rattling scales. "According to

my kin, she was taken by Raphael. No one has seen either of them since he absconded with her."

"Who the fuck is he?" Abria demanded.

"An archangel," I told her, "but one who signed on with Satan."

"Did we come all this way for nothing? Where is he?"

Hysteria trod close to the surface. I heard it in her voice and sent calm winging her way.

Roya shambled toward me and fell to one knee. "Forgive me, Regent. I have failed you."

"Get up," I said gruffly. "You did not fail."

"But I was supposed to keep Tiana safe. They ripped her from me."

Because she didn't show any signs of rising, I grabbed her arms and pulled her to her feet. "Not your fault," I repeated. "We'll figure this out."

"We did our part," Nidhogg stated. "We would see you home."

"I'm not leaving without Tiana," Abria cried.

"She's not here." Nidhogg took on a patient tone, much as he might have used with a young dragon.

"We don't know that," Abria insisted.

"You have half an hour," Nidhogg told me. "Determine if you want to return of if we leave you."

Gwydion, Arianrhod, and Ceridwen ambled over. "Seems like a wasted journey," Gwydion said.

"Perhaps not," Arianrhod spoke up and stared pointedly at Ceridwen.

The seer rolled her eyes. "Fine. I admit I once knew

Raphael rather well, but it does not mean I know where to find him."

"Can you try?" Abria clasped her hands together. "Please."

Ceridwen narrowed her eyes. "Aye, but don't get your hopes up. That one has many homes."

I started to tell her to begin with the ones closest to our current location but had the wisdom to remain silent. She'd agreed to help.

It would have to be enough.

"Wait here," I told Abria and returned to tell Breanne to keep the army together so they could return when the dragons were ready to leave. I'd stay put until I found my daughter—no matter how long it took.

If we had to fight our way through Hell, so be it. At least I wouldn't sacrifice my people. Breanne wouldn't agree, but she was bound to obey me. We could argue it up one side and down the other—back in Faery.

CHAPTER 16
TIANA

Shudders wracked my body. I sucked air like a blacksmith's bellows working to calm myself. The person I wanted to project was calm, cool, collected, and that was so not happening.

"What are these conditions?" Raphael's "nice" face shifted to the "mean" one.

I forced words past my clattering teeth. "I will accept your offer, but I must return to my home, to Underhill, two months out of each year."

I don't know quite what I'd expected, but he threw back his head and laughed uproariously as if I'd told the richest of jokes.

"And if I refuse?" His tone was dangerously smooth.

"Then so do I." I wrapped my arms around my torso.

"I do not require your acquiescence. I can force you to my will."

I stood straight. "I don't believe you. If that were true, we wouldn't be having this discussion."

His hand snaked out. Before he struck me, I gritted. "That's a dealbreaker too. I'm nobody's punching bag."

I expected him to slap me anyway. He didn't. What in the unholy hell? What could I possible have that he wanted so badly?

"I gave you an opportunity," he sneered. "You could have been comfortable. See how you like the alternative. I'll be back in a dozen years—perhaps two dozen—to see if you've rethought things."

"What do you mean about being back? Where are you going?"

Almost before I got the words out, I was falling, tumbling down a pitch-black shaft, and banging against the walls. I reached for a mage light, but the magic I'd thought was back deserted me.

I fell for a long time. Hours. Days. If I didn't fight them, the collisions with the walls didn't hurt as much. I withdrew into myself. Would I fall forever? Until Raphael chose to show up again?

I pitched up against something hard enough to knock the breath out of me. Was my reprieve temporary? Had I hit a ledge or something? Not expecting much, I tried to kindle a mage light again.

It didn't exactly blaze to life, but at least it took shape casting a pallid yellow glow over my surroundings. Caves had become an overarching motif in my life these days. This one was small, maybe two meters across. Foul-smelling water dripped down the walls. There was no place dry to sit, so not much reason to move from the place I'd fallen.

The floor was smooth, wet dirt. The walls studded with sharp rocks. If I got desperate, I'd chance the water, but there was no food. What effect did starvation have on immortality? It hadn't been part of any of my lessons, or if it had, I wasn't paying attention.

I crawled to where I could lean my battered body against a wall. If I considered the prospect of being here for years, I'd lose it. Start screaming and never stop.

"Don't be stupid," I said out loud to hear something, anything, but the echoing silence of my surroundings.

Magic is like any other commodity. It requires food and rest to operate at peak efficiency. I hadn't depleted mine, but it wouldn't last in the face of starvation. I had no idea if I had any moves left, but if I did, I needed to roll them out sooner rather than later.

I also had to be smart and methodical. I couldn't afford to blow through power hunting for solutions. Raphael wouldn't have chucked me somewhere I could teleport out of. No reason to squander magic on that front.

If I couldn't teleport out of my prison, was there another escape hatch? I'd never find out if I didn't look. Beginning at ground level, I explored every centimeter of the wall surface. I hadn't expected to find anything, and I didn't. One out-of-the-way corner yielded a pile of bones. I should have left it at that, but no. I had to look at them.

Clearly, I wasn't the first prisoner in this cell. On closer inspection, the bones appeared human. Why bother to dump mortals here when they could be killed outright so easily?

I hunkered over the bones hoping they'd speak to me. They didn't. All I figured out was they weren't all that old. When I grew desperate, I could crack them against a rock and suck on the marrow.

"I will not be here that long," I announced and straightened.

No resources at ground level. What about farther up? Raphael knew I could fly, but perhaps he assumed I'd be so demoralized I'd sink into a heap of remorse anxious for his return. For all I knew, he was watching from some arcane perch and laughing his head off just like when I'd said I intended to spend time in Underhill each year.

Flying doesn't require magic. Careful not to injure my wings in such close quarters, I spread them and flew straight up until I was about thirty meters above the ground. From there, I hovered and turned to inspect the walls.

I had no idea what I hunted, but even if I flapped to the top of the shaft, I was pretty sure I wouldn't return to the luxurious room I'd been ejected from. Done exploring the current level, I fluttered another thirty meters up and tried again.

I had nothing but time. My only limiting factor was the pain in my shoulders from remaining airborne. I tried every trick I knew and visualized striking pay dirt. There had to be a way out of here. No one would construct something like this without a secondary way out. What if the main structure collapsed?

Kirwan accused me of being lazy. He'd been right, but he'd also never challenged me with a task where my survival depended on getting it right. Back in Underhill, I'd been convinced the Sidhe were my biggest problem, that if I could only break loose from them, my life would improve dramatically.

What a fool I'd been. If the goddess granted me grace—and a second chance—I'd fall all over myself apologizing.

Because I was tired, I almost missed the place my mage light reflected differently. It was subtle, and I'm still not sure what drew me back to the spot that was 99 percent like every other nook and cranny I'd evaluated during my upward transit.

My heart pounded; breath came fast.

"It's probably nothing," I muttered, not wanting the crash when some weird abnormality promised hope where none existed. Twisting, I flapped a bit higher and found an opening in all that endless rock and dirt. If nothing else, it would be a place to rest my weary wings.

The notch was narrow, so slender I folded my wings and muscled my way through. For a few moments, it was nip and tuck. Nothing to grab hold of, so I teetered on the edge, almost falling backward into the abyss. My hands and feet scrabbled against dirt that refused to offer purchase. Slithering, panting, and grabbing one precarious hold after the next, I finally ended up facedown sucking dust into my tired lungs.

I had no idea if this was a dead end or my ticket out of here, but at least I wasn't flying any longer. My shoulder blades were on fire. Other muscles I'd never so much as noticed felt like they were a thousand years old.

I lay there for longer than I should have, mostly because I was afraid I'd done all this work for nothing. That I'd walk into a dead end and be forced to begin my search anew.

Inertia was getting me nowhere fast. I shoved to my feet. Once I'd made it through the narrow opening, there was plenty of space to stand upright. When I played my mage light over what lay ahead, it was more of the same. Dirt and rocks, but instead of a cave, this was a tunnel. And it was dry.

It had to lead somewhere, so I trudged along it grateful not to hear gates clanking shut behind me. Maybe Raphael wasn't watching over me like I'd thought. If so, he'd have found ways to fuck with my head.

The passageway twisted and turned, but it climbed too. After a few hundred feet, I dared to hope I was moving toward an opening from my underground prison. Bones littered the path, growing more prevalent as I moved higher. Maybe the ones I'd found below belonged to unfortunates who'd fallen through the hole and crashed to the bottom.

Made sense. Mortals didn't have mage lights, so they'd have been running blind. My nose twitched as an unfamiliar scent wafted my way. Was it the outside world, or some outside world since it was a sure bet I wasn't on Earth.

I stopped and inhaled, sorting what lay ahead. I was making progress—I thought. No point ruining it by waltzing into something unanticipated. Like a guardian at the gates.

My mind played over possibilities. If I'd paid closer

attention to my studies, I'd have had a better idea which monsters preferred this type of environment.

Blerg. "If I'd paid closer attention" was a recurring theme as if the universe was doling out punishment for my desultory performance as a student.

The smell was definitely rank as I sampled it. If I augmented my hearing with magic, I detected rolling snorts, as if whatever it was was in pain.

I rocked from foot to foot. Either I retreated to my starting point, or I moved forward. There hadn't been any side channels, and I'd checked carefully. The snorts changed to moans.

I started forward. Maybe the monster—or whatever it was—was a prisoner just like me. If we could help each other...

Determined to face my fears rather than be hamstrung by indecision, I forged ahead. The moans grew louder accompanied by labored breathing. I should have been afraid, but I was more apprehensive about retracing my steps.

I knew what lay behind me: a slow withering fueled by putrid water and no food. What lay ahead was an unknown. It might be worse, but I doubted it.

I've never been one to dither or second-guess. No one has ever accused me of overthinking anything. After clearing my mind of everything but my next step, I plodded forward.

Half a dozen twists and turns later, light streamed through, illuminating my path. I killed my mage light and picked up the pace. Nothing had jumped out to stop me. It argued I'd find some kind of barrier ahead.

Sure enough, iron bars came into view.

Behind them stood a battered griffon. His lion fur had sloughed off in big patches as if he had mange. The eagle portion was partially devoid of feathers. He tried to roar, but it came out as a pathetic squeal.

He blinked at me out of his lidless avian eyes. I stared back. The smell from his cage was atrocious, but the poor thing was stuck. No food. No water that I could see.

I licked dry lips and walked forward until I could curl my fingers around the bars.

His beak clacked. "You can touch them?" he croaked. His voice sounded rusty as if he hadn't used it in a long while.

"Yeah. Um, why are you here?"

He tossed his feathered head. "Same question back your way."

I started to remind him he was the one in a cage, but I felt sorry for him. "I displeased Raphael, so he chucked me in a pit." I jerked a thumb over one shoulder in the general direction I'd come from.

The griffon drew back until he was pressed against the opposite bars and turned his head away.

What had I said that made him shut down?

I tried again. "Are you Raphael's prisoner too?"

"Go away."

I eyed the cage. It created a barrier across the passageway. I could fly over it, but I didn't want to leave my new friend by himself.

Eh, *new friend* was stretching it. I might want to be his friend, but my paltry attempts at communication had turned him off cold. Spreading my wings, I flew over the top and landed on the other side, the one he was plastered against.

From the looks of the light, it wasn't far to the surface, whatever that meant. "Do you know where we are?" I asked.

He'd backed away but turned to shoot an incredulous glance my way. "If you're associated with Rafael, you know the answer to that question. Don't play games with me. I'm not in the mood."

Aho. I saw the problem. After clasping my hands in front of me, I said, "My name is Tiana Cardassier. My father is Elwyn Cardassier, regent to the Sidhe. My mother is Abria MacLeone. She's an animal mage. I carry both magics."

He'd taken a step closer. "With that lineage, what are you doing with Raphael?"

"I was kidnapped by Leviathans along with another Sidhe. Raphael showed up and whisked me away. When I didn't instantly agree with his plans for me, he dumped me in a cave to contemplate my insolence—or something."

"I see. Do you have enough magic to pry my cage open?"

I started to say yes, but rash decisions hadn't bought me much. "First, tell me who you are and how you ended up here."

He bobbed his head. "Fair enough. I don't suppose you have any water."

"Sorry. No."

"My people have had little to do since Apollo and Nemesis faded from view. No chariots to pull, no crowds to cheer us on. Many of us were lost when Atlantis fell. Those who remained ended up in a remote corner of—"

"Not that I'm not interested," I interrupted, "but we may not have much time."

"Pfft." More beak clacks. "You're the first person I've seen in forever."

"Yeah, but Raphael could be keeping an eye on me."

The griffon rolled his shoulders amid creaking noises. "My mate grew weary of our domain. She flew farther and farther afield searching for a new spot for our pride. One day, she didn't return."

His neck drooped. "I searched through borderworld after borderworld. Finally, I changed tactics and hunted through Hell. It was the only place left."

"Found her, huh?"

"Aye. She'd been imprisoned by Raphael and a few other bastards. I traded her freedom for my own."

My throat tightened. Rage at Raphael seared me. I wanted to rip him to shreds with my bare hands. Funneling my fury, I sent a laser jet of power and sliced through three bars. They clattered to the ground.

The griffon tried to squeeze through, but the hole wasn't quite big enough. A couple more cuts fixed that little problem. He squeezed past and lumbered up the passageway toward the light source.

I stared after him. "No thanks yous?"

"Thank you, Tiana," floated back to me.

I hurried to catch up. We were stronger together. Why didn't he recognize that? His scent changed from rank animal to clean, pure magic. I ran faster. He was planning to teleport. I'd bet my ass on it.

"Take me with you," I panted from four meters back.

He stopped and spun to face me. "I can't."

"Why not?"

"Well, isn't this just sweet," a familiar voice snarled. Raphael oozed through from nowhere and stood with his wings outstretched. No portal, no nothing.

I closed the distance to the griffon and prepared to fight. There were two of us now. Maybe laughable odds against an archangel, but at least I wasn't alone.

The griffon spread his wings and roared. "Never again."

"We'll see about that."

Raphael's laughter was the last thing I heard before rockfall drowned it out. Boulders crashed on us from every angle. The griffon snaked out a taloned foot and dragged me under his body.

I built warding. It wasn't perfect, but it deflected the worst of the battering designed to crush the life out of us.

"You must find my mate," he wheezed. "Her name is Crine. Tell her what happened to me."

"Sure, but we're not dead yet," I replied.

Somewhere out there my parents were hunting for me along with the whole of the Sidhe army. I opened my mind voice and shouted as loud as I could for whoever was close enough to hear me.

CHAPTER 17

ABRIA

My mind churned through ideas, discarding them as quickly as they surfaced. I'd been so certain once we found the Leviathans, we'd find Tiana. Why hadn't she stayed with her captors?

Talk about a stupid question.

Give it a break. She did the same thing I would have. She's been trying to escape since she was taken.

"Can I do anything?" Roya asked. Her brow was pinched with worry. She still blamed herself, but none of this was remotely her fault. I'd already said as much. Guilt is a funny thing, though. It's tough to wade through to the other side of it.

I shook my head. "There's something I'm missing. I have to figure out what it is."

Roya placed a hand on my arm. "I had time, so I used my magic to map what I could of this quadrant of Hell."

A series of images cascaded through my mind. Level

after level of endless cracked red earth with an occasional cave to break the monotony. What I didn't see were demons.

"No one lives here?" I met her gaze.

"Doesn't appear so, but they could have cloaked themselves."

I shook my head. "Why would they bother? They wouldn't expect an intrusion or have sensed your inspection."

"I was careful," she agreed. "If anyone had apprehended me, they'd have shut me down fast, and it never happened."

Blake joined us. "It's settled," he said. "Breanne and the army will return to Underhill with a dragon escort whenever they're ready to leave. Odin and Hel will remain along with a few Valkyries, but the rest of his force will leave as well."

"What about the Celts?" I asked.

"Unknown." He bit off the word, which told me how pissed off he was.

"We're staying," I said not making it into a question. No reason to. I was not returning emptyhanded.

He nodded. "Aye. Until we find Tiana—or have solid reasons to believe she's not anywhere close—we shall remain."

I tallied up who'd be left once the bulk of the Sidhe and Norse armies left. It wasn't encouraging. We wouldn't have the manpower to deal with a concerted—

My head snapped around. "Did you hear that?" I demanded.

"Hear what?" Roya asked.

"Ssht." Blake cocked his head to one side, listening intently.

I threw my third ear wide open, augmenting its ability with magic. Yes! There it was again. "It's Tiana. I know it," I crowed.

Blake straightened. "I think so too, but it might be a trap."

"Set by whom?" I demanded. "The Leviathans are on their way to dragon hell." Or somewhere. I hadn't figured out what Nidhogg and Dewi planned to do with their lowlife kinsmen. It wasn't my problem. I had plenty without borrowing new ones.

"We'll find out soon enough." Power shimmered around Blake as he prepared to home in on the location of Tiana's cries for help.

"Hang on," I said. "I'm anxious to find her too, but we need more of us."

"I heard that." Cailleach hurried forward.

"Me too," Arianrhod said and stopped dead in her tracks. "Danu's breath. Is that Tiana bellowing?"

"We think so," Blake replied and went back to breathing life into a tracking spell.

"Gwydion. Bran." Arianrhod yelled so loud it hurt my ears. Why in the hell hadn't she used telepathy?

Dewi half flew, half lumbered near with the master enchanter still firmly on her back. "We're preparing to depart—" she started before her eyes whirled faster. "Found her, eh? Good news, indeed. What are we waiting for?"

"I'm building a tracking spell," Blake explained.

"Pfft. No need. I'll take you to her." The dragon's enchantment crackled around us, sweeping us into its maw. I assumed it would include everyone who stood nearby.

"We're coming," Odin thundered.

Off to my right, he and Nidhogg flickered into view.

So much for my concerns we'd be outmanned and outgunned. A couple of dragons were a match for damn near anything. Because I could hear Tiana—and her mind voice grew louder and more strident as Dewi's spell moved us closer—I assumed the teleport would be over in a matter of minutes.

Not so.

Perhaps half an hour ticked past before the crash of rockfall drowned out my daughter's mindspeech. We emerged in a narrow passageway choked with boulders crashing down from above. I pivoted to avoid a direct hit, once and again. Roya leapt atop a boulder and rode it to the ground.

"That's about enough," Dewi trumpeted. Rocks stopped midair, floating quietly to resting places. No more fell.

Breath streamed from me. Once my power wakened, I was strong, but I'd give damn near anything for a tenth of Dewi's talent. She'd stopped a rockslide without apparent effort.

Nidhogg swung his snout this way and that until he focused on a point off to my left. Peering through slitted eyes, I made out a shadowy figure with enormous, outstretched wings.

Fire spewed from the black dragon, to be joined by more flames from Dewi. The figure, presumably Raphael, hopped this way and that. Water poured from somewhere dousing his wings.

"You trespass," blasted through my head.

"Minor compared with kidnapping," Blake shouted back.

I scanned the passageway floor, hunting for Tiana. Would this be another dead end? Another instance of, "She was here, but another son of a bitch nasty god took off with her."

The dragons didn't back off. Fire flowed in a steady stream. Gwydion and Odin jumped from their perches and marched toward Raphael's position atop a substantial boulder.

Surely, he knew he couldn't walk away from this unscathed, yet there he stood. A staff materialized in Gwydion's hand. A thing of beauty, it blazed blue-white as he leveled it at Raphael. Power crackled from its tip; lightning bolts followed. Bran used his bulk to pick up boulders and heave them at the archangel.

Between fire, lightning, and boulders, the men and dragons had it covered.

I broke away from the group with Roya, Cailleach, and Arianrhod flanking me. Together, we searched every pile of rocks. Tiana wasn't screeching any longer. Had the whole thing been a charade designed by Raphael to throw us off the true track?

"Tiana." I yelled.

"Use magic," Arianrhod said dryly. "It's faster."

It pains me to admit it, but she was right. I activated a tracking spell; it lit right away. Ducking, weaving, and jumping over debris, I ran toward a distant heap of jagged rocks. The goddess, the witch, and Roya helped me toss them aside.

Between brute force and magic, we worked our way down to a tawny patch of fur barely clinging to life. I had no idea what it was, but I stroked its rough hide sending love and light through my touch.

Across the cavern from us, a battle still raged. Smoke and ash made it tough to breathe and even harder to see.

After we'd moved a few more rocks, the fur turned out to be a griffon. Where in the hell had he come from?

Tiana had to be here. My magic ran true when my own blood was at stake. I couldn't have made a mistake of that magnitude.

"She's underneath," Arianrhod said. "And out cold. Hang on." Vibrant threads of power dove beneath the griffon's limp body.

A feeble moan was followed by another that broke my heart. I'd spent the last twelve years protecting my child from, well, from everything. Despite her highhanded ways, she'd been innocent.

No more. The past few days had erased a lifetime of being wrapped in a protective bubble. I bit my lower lip hard enough to draw blood. I'd do whatever it took to put the pieces back together, to restore my daughter's confidence in a benevolent world.

Oh really? one of my caustic inner voices piped up. *You were part of the problem, and you have another chance. Don't fuck it up.*

Tiana chose than moment to crawl out from beneath the griffon and into my arms. Her moans turned to sobs so violent her whole body shook. "Help him, Momma," she gasped out. "He saved me."

It took a moment for me to understand she meant the griffon, but Arianrhod was already working on him. Power crackled from her fingertips as she breathed energy and magic into his inert form.

I rocked Tiana against me, vowing never to let her out of my sight again. I didn't want to turn her into a prisoner, but never having to worry where she was held undeniable appeal. Her pretty green wings had turned almost black, and her face was ravaged. Nothing of its former childlike softness remained.

A lesser, more malleable youth might not have survived.

She wriggled, twisting so she could see the goddess and the griffon. "Will he be all right?" she stammered. "He has to be. I couldn't stand it if he died." More sobs. "Raphael captured his mate, Momma. He traded his freedom for hers. You have to save him so he can find Crine again."

"Yes, child. Hush." I stroked her filthy, tangled hair. "Arianrhod has it under control."

Tiana sagged against me. Cailleach rubbed her shoulders.

The griffon came to life under Arianrhod's ministrations. Beak clacks and purring told me he'd survive to fight another day. I wanted to know how he'd ended up here—or how his mate had. The one he'd willingly gone into servitude to save. Like many birds, they pair bonded for life, but he'd paid a heavy price for his devotion.

Tiana wriggled out of my embrace, crawled to the griffon, and threw her arms around his neck. "Thank you for protecting me."

"You broke the bars of my prison. How could I have done less?"

A high-pitched yelp from across the cave was followed by several more. When I straightened, the place Raphael had stood was a pyre three meters high. Dragonfire had finally made an end of him.

Good riddance.

"Is he really gone?" Tiana pointed at the flames.

"For now," Arianrhod said.

"But not forever," Roya tossed out. "His kind have more than nine lives. Satan will see that he's resurrected soon."

Tiana gasped, let go of the griffon, and twirled to face the changeling. When Roya opened her arms, Tiana dove into them, hugging her close. "Aw geez. You're all right. I was so worried they'd do something bad to you after Rafael made off with me."

Roya held her, crooning wordlessly. "Never saw a soul after you left." Letting go, she tipped Tiana's chin upward to meet her gaze. "I was plenty worried too. I should have done more—"

"What could you have done?" Tiana demanded. "There were too many of them, and they were strong. So strong."

She shivered but didn't say anything more. She didn't have to. The Leviathans were out of the equation, but whenever Raphael resurfaced, she'd be squarely in his gunsights. By then, she'd have a few more years under her belt.

And a whole lot more skills, if she got over her allergy to doing what she was told.

The griffon settled his haunches beneath him. "Many

thanks to you all," he said. "If it's all the same to you, I'll be on my way."

"But where can I find you?" Tiana's voice cracked. More tears followed.

He bent his head. New feathers were already filling in the bald spots. "You have no need to find me, young mage."

"What if I want to?"

I rocked back on my heels and followed the exchange. Tiana's headstrong nature hadn't altered; it worried me. Had she learned nothing from this experience?

"Call me," the griffon was saying. "I will come to you if I'm able."

"But I don't know your name."

He hesitated before bending and whispering something into her ear. "I am trusting you, young mage. Names have power, and you will hold mine close, never sharing it with another."

"I promise," she said without hesitation but then looked confused. "You told me your mate's name."

He clacked his beak. "Not the real one."

His form took on an incandescent aspect before it vanished from sight. I stared after him. Dragons could teleport in and out of this spot; apparently, so could griffons.

Blake loped into view and snatched Tiana into his arms, hugging her until she whimpered. When he let go, he set her down and said, "You will never pull another stunt like that. Do we understand one another?"

I expected her to mouth off and tell him she'd been the victim here. She didn't. Instead, she nodded solemnly, said, "Yes, Father," and folded her hands in front of her.

He clanked a truth spell over her and repeated his question. Tiana didn't flinch or engage in her usual barrage of snide comments.

Soot smeared Blake's face. Burned spots still smoldered in his heavy jacket. New lines scribed his forehead and around his eyes. He'd been far more worried than he let on. When we got out of here, I'd have to ask him what he'd expected to find.

Or not. It wasn't the best idea. We needed to move forward, not wallow in the hideous outcomes we might have unearthed. I sent a sidelong glance at my daughter. She stood quietly. She had to be exhausted, but that had never stopped her from tacking a spiteful remark onto nearly everything.

Cailleach nudged me and murmured, *"This is looking promising,"* in shielded telepathy.

It was, but would it last?

Rocks crashed against one another. I stiffened and readied power. Had we missed something? Did Raphael have minions?

The passageway was still cloudy with ash and smoke. Peering through the murk, I saw Nidhogg and Dewi wading toward us through the wreckage and chucking rocks aside to clear a path.

Tiana made a strangled sound. "Those are dragons."

She'd never seen one other than in pictures, so of course, she'd be trapped between awe, fascination, and fear. They can be quite imposing.

"Many lent their magic to save you, child," Blake informed her.

"But dragons?" She raised her green eyes to stare at her father. "Was it because of the Leviathans?"

"What do you think?" he asked her.

Tiana turned and faced the approaching dragons. Nidhogg was in the lead. When he drew close, she fell to one knee and bowed her head. "Thank you so much for helping to free me," she said in her clear, ringing child's voice.

"What about me?" Dewi huffed steam; it billowed around Tiana's kneeling form.

My daughter raised her head but remained in a crouch. "Of course, you too. You are beautiful. Like images in the scrolls in our library, but so much more vibrant. Your scales glisten in the light."

"It's good to be appreciated." Dewi puffed more smoke.

Blake hooked an arm under Tiana's shoulder and hauled her upright. "Good start," he murmured, "but there are others who are deserving of your undying devotion."

Tiana turned to Arianrhod and bowed. "I apologize for being such a brat and disparaging your hospitality when you offered me a roof in Caer Sidi."

The goddess trained her bi-colored eyes on Tiana. "Accepted. Perhaps your next visit will be less eventful."

"I hope so," Tiana said. "I'm evented out." Turning to Cailleach, she bowed and said, "Thank you for always being there for Mother. And for me. I am sorry for causing so much trouble."

"I do believe you mean that, child." Cailleach patted her cheek.

"You're not done," Blake prodded.

I started to tell him to lay off, but our daughter needed to be accountable—to everyone.

She nodded and glanced at the small circle of mages around her. "I do not know most of your names, but thank you for taking the time and magic to rescue me. After I freed the griffon, I had no idea what lay ahead—or if I had the skill to get myself out of Raphael's clutches."

Ceridwen plopped into our midst. "Never did find that bastard," she announced, "but it appears you managed without my help." After dropping a hand onto Tiana's shoulder, she asked, "What did he want from you?"

I'd planned to find that out, but only after my daughter was back in Underhill. "Tiana needs rest—" I began.

"It's okay, Momma," she said. "This won't take long. Raphael wanted me for his bride. Not right away but when I got a little older."

"Did he say what the two of you would do?" Ceridwen pressed.

"Rule together over maybe the Leviathans. That part wasn't very clear."

The goddess leaned close. "Did he touch you, child?"

My heart twisted. Good thing Ceridwen was asking the tough questions, ones I might never have gotten around to.

Tiana shook her head. "Not in the way you mean. He grabbed my shoulder, but he didn't do...anything else."

"Thank Danu." Ceridwen straightened.

"What did you see in that kettle of yours?" Blake demanded.

"Two futures. Had he claimed her with more than

words, we'd be facing a far more worrisome set of problems."

Tiana crab-walked to me. I wrapped an arm around her shoulders. Ceridwen's pronouncement had chilled me. No doubt it shocked Tiana.

"No reason to remain here any longer," Nidhogg growled in his deep voice.

I bowed low. "May I join my daughter and offer heartfelt thanks for your assistance."

"I propose a feast," Odin bellowed. "I will host everyone in Asgard."

"Deal." Blake beamed. "But first, we must stop in Underhill to clean up and change."

"Not a problem. It will take me a while to get everything set up," the Norse god said.

"I assume the feast includes dragons." Nidhogg swung his head around and batted Odin.

"Aye. Plenty of space—lots of spare sheep—and the frost giants have been asking after you for a long time."

"At least three sheep for each dragon." Nidhogg had fallen into bargaining mode.

"Take five. The herds need thinning."

I wasn't exactly in a festive mood. I wanted to retire to Underhill with my family, hold them close, and sleep for days. Still, it wasn't right not to pay homage to those who'd helped us.

Blake was far more skilled than me when it came to the care and nurturing of allies.

I wasn't sure how, but we transitioned from the passageway to the spot the Sidhe and Norse armies milled about. Hedrek was there, deep in conversation with Breanne. I'd wondered what happened to him. Once everyone was in one spot, the dragons spun their magic and transported us to Asgard.

After a few goodbyes and see-you-soons, Blake crafted a journey spell that took Tiana, Roya, Cailleach, and me to Underhill.

Following her polite round of thank-yous, Tiana had been uncharacteristically silent. When we were finally alone in our suite of rooms, she caught my hand and called after Blake who'd headed for the shower.

"Aye." He raised a dark brow once he stood across from her. "Not much time. Can this wait?"

She shook her head. Color flooded her dirty face. "I am sorry I caused everyone so much trouble. I will do my best to mend my ways."

"I'm sure you will." I smiled encouragingly.

Blake waved me to silence. "Don't let her off the hook. She isn't done."

"You're right," Tiana agreed. "I'm not. I've been perfectly horrible these past few years. Reckless. Spoiled. Difficult. If you didn't give me what I wanted, I threw tantrums." She dropped her gaze to the floor. "I'm ashamed of myself."

"You feel bad now," Blake told her. "The trick will be whether this newfound remorse sticks with you a month from now. Or a year. It won't be easy, Tiana. You've developed patterns that aren't productive."

"You'll help me, right?" In a flash of her old self, she grinned.

"If by help, you mean a good swift boot in the ass, then aye, I'll help."

I looked from one to the other. They'd run down. "Go clean up," I told Tiana. "We leave in half an hour."

Once she was gone, I murmured to Blake, "Tough love, eh?"

"She needs it," he said gruffly. "Part of this isn't her fault. We should have held her accountable long since."

I forced myself to stare into his dark eyes and nod acquiescence. His message was clear. No more excuses for my errant spawn. No more pampering. From today on, her childhood was formally over.

"Makes me sad," I murmured.

"She couldn't remain a child forever," he reminded me. "Come on. We need to ready ourselves for Odin's hospitality."

I trailed after him. Once we hit the bedroom, I tossed clothes this way and that. When I joined him in the shower, I wrapped my arms around him and lost myself in his enticing scent, his alluring body, and his love.

CHAPTER 18
BLAKE

My family was whole again. Joy ignited every nerve ending like a fine old whiskey until I felt buoyant. Tiana had learned something. Whether the lessons stuck remained to be seen, but I refused to allow uncertainty about the future to dampen my delight in how the day turned out.

We hadn't put either army at risk.

Dragons had ruled the field.

The Sidhe-Norse alliance was stronger than it had been.

I dared hope we'd see a few more dragons in the years to come.

Tiana's experience had marked her, changed her wings to nearly the shade of mine absent their colorful inserts. Her face was thinner, the playful roundness gone. I could envision the woman she'd grow into...

"You're a million kilometers away." Abria threaded her

arms around me and crushed her naked body against mine, her intention crystal clear.

"You're just the one to call me back."

"Oh, am I now?" She licked water off my neck and ran her nails down my back.

Between us, my cock rose to fullness. Suddenly, whether we were late getting back to Asgard paled to insignificance. I lowered my mouth to Abria's and kissed her hard.

The kiss turned endless as we drank each other in. Even though I've kissed her thousands of times, each new kiss is more exciting than the very first time I buried my tongue in her mouth. My heart hammered against my ribs; passion engulfed me until the only thing in the world was water pounding down on me and the woman in my arms.

She bit my lower lip; I bit back, and then I turned her so she was spreadeagled against the marble lining the bathroom. She arched her back. The motion raised her buttocks, separating them to display her sex.

Spiky red curls streamed with water. Stabilizing myself with my hands over hers, I plunged into her. Nothing elegant. Just pure, sweet lust as I thrust deep and fast.

She dissolved around me; I hung on and dialed up the intensity. I may have cheated with magic, but why have it if you don't use it?

Two climaxes later, she jackknifed out from under me and fell to her knees, taking me into her mouth. The feel of her mouth and hands is indescribable. Abria is endlessly inventive. I can never anticipate what she'll do next.

After a thorough tonguing up one side and down the other, she took most of me into her mouth, scraping her teeth up my shaft. My balls were so tight, they'd passed the point of pain. Still I held on, not wanting the sharp, exquisite sensations to end.

Not only is my mate inventive. She cheats. Something twitched its way into my anus, something magical. When it teased the back of my prostate, control fled, and semen juddered from me.

She swallowed every drop and then cleaned me with her tongue.

Both of us sucked air in panting gulps. I drew her to her feet and held her close as our bodies quieted.

"We should get dressed," Abria murmured. "Tiana will wonder what happened to us."

"No, she won't," I said. "She's still in good girl mode."

Abria drew back. "You don't expect it to last?"

I turned the water off and tossed her a towel as I considered her question. "Some of it will," I said at last. "She'll never be anyone's lackey."

"We'll stay on top of it. Only thing we can do." Abria wrapped her wet hair in a towel and walked toward the bedroom.

I joined her and dredged up something appropriate for a Sidhe regent to wear to a victory celebration. In this instance, I chose buff-colored leather trousers, a full-sleeved dark-blue shirt, and a ceremonial tunic embossed with runic markings symbolic of my rank.

"Will this do?" Abria glided into my line of vision. A long black silk sheath clung to her breasts and hips. She'd tied a teal sash around her waist. A black woolen cape edged with leather completed her outfit. She'd dragged her damp hair into a queue that rode low on her neck with tendrils curling around her face.

I stopped dead, breath catching in my throat. "You are the most incredible, the most gorgeous—"

She laughed and waved me to silence. "I get the picture. Shall I wear the emerald, or is it overkill?"

In answer, I retrieved the five-carat stone suspended from a golden chain from its velvet-lined box and hung it around her neck. Next I handed her matching earrings.

She threaded them through her ears, and then sat on the bed to slip her feet into flat pumps.

Shoes. I knew I'd forgotten something and retrieved a soft, worn pair of leather loafers from an armoire.

Arm in arm, we left our room intent on grabbing Tiana and leaving.

She sat on a sofa in the living room with tears streaking her face. A bruise had darkened on one cheek. When she saw us, she sprang to her feet.

Abria hurried to her. "What's wrong, darling?"

"More like what's not right," she retorted. "My wings look like they took a bath in soot." She pinched her thin cheeks. "I'm not pretty anymore. Maybe I could stay here. I don't want anyone to see me like this."

More tears rolled down her face, but she stood tall, not giving in to sobs.

"How about a more festive outfit," I suggested.

"Not going to help my wings—or my face."

I closed the distance to her and grabbed one arm. "Stop feeling sorry for yourself. You're alive. It could have been so much worse."

"I don't mean to be ungrateful, but I can't help how I feel." She shook her head. "Something isn't right. I thought I'd be better once I was home."

"You will be." I softened my tone. "Give it time. You've been through a lot."

"Hope you're right, Daddy."

My heart cracked open. She hadn't called me that since she'd been around five. I held her close, soothing her with a calming spell.

Abria hustled down the hall toward Tiana's room. When she returned, she had a floral robe slung over one arm and a pair of silver sandals. "Let's put these on," she said briskly. "And then we'll get going."

While the women were engaged in a quick wardrobe change, I poured mead into three glasses. Nothing like a small ceremony to lift flagging sprits. When I returned with my bounty, Tiana did look perkier. Trading her black pants and shirt for something colorful had been a good idea.

I handed her a glass and another to Abria. Raising mine, I said, "I propose a toast to Tiana."

Her green eyes widened in surprise.

"Aye, to Tiana," Abria said. "To her bravery and spirit."

"She never gave up," I added and raised my tumbler to my lips.

After one quick swallow and a pucker-face when the alcohol burned her tongue and throat, Tiana asked, "Is that how you really see me?"

"In this instance, yes," I told her.

"Keep making good decisions," Abria told our daughter.

"Time to go," I said to my brood and summoned the power to transport us to Asgard.

Festivities were in full swing when we popped out. Odin loped over and slapped me across the back. It took all my willpower not to stagger under the blow.

He whistled shrilly; a Valkyrie swooped down and handed mugs of something foamy and alcoholic to Abria and me.

"Does she get one?" Odin pointed at Tiana.

Before I could reply, my daughter said, "Thank you, but not for me. We had mead before leaving home."

Abria's brows shot up. Both of us were well aware of our daughter sneaking adult beverages. Perhaps it was only interesting if it was forbidden.

Odin skewered Tiana with his single eye. Something must have caught his attention because he walked closer and dropped a hand on her shoulder. "Are you all right, missy?"

"Not really. Father says it will pass."

Abria edged nearer Odin and Tiana, clearly not trusting his intentions. I didn't, either, but even Odin probably drew the line at taking advantage of children.

He glared my way; maybe he'd read my thoughts. "Do you mind if I have a closer look?"

"At what?" Abria's tone was chilly. She set her tumbler on the ground.

"I'll be all right." Tiana ducked from beneath Odin's grip. "Thank you for your concern, though."

She started to walk toward tables piled high with food.

"Not so fast," Odin bellowed.

The old Tiana would have kept on walking, but she stopped dead. And then I saw a bluish light extending between her and the Norse god.

"Leave her alone," I growled. "She's been through enough."

Abria shot power of her own at Odin's beam—or whatever it was—but didn't make a dent. "Why are you holding her against her will?" Abria demanded.

A crowd was gathering. My first inclination was to open another journey spell and hightail it back to Underhill. It wouldn't fix whatever was playing out, though. All it would do was put it off.

"What did you see?" I asked Odin.

"Not sure," he growled, "but 'tis best to get ahead of these things."

"What things?"

Odin reeled in his enchantment. Tiana turned and walked toward him with jerky, puppet-like steps. "What happened when you were with Raphael?" Odin asked softly. I hadn't known he was capable of speaking so gently.

Tiana's eyes widened. For the briefest of moments, they whirled like dragon eyes. But I might have imagined it. Her tongue snaked out.

Ceridwen materialized next to Odin. "I already asked if he touched you. Did you eat or drink anything he offered?"

Tiana nodded. When she opened her mouth, she stammered, "Leviathans drank my blood too."

"What did you eat?" I asked, afraid of her answer, but needing to know.

"S-sweetmeats and mead."

Abria grabbed hold of my arm. *"Is this as bad as I fear?"*

"Possibly." I downplayed my worries, so Abria didn't throw her body over Tiana's and whisk her away. I should have examined her once we were in Underhill. I hadn't because I needed her to be whole.

"What's going on?" Nidhogg lumbered to where we stood. "We won. Why is everyone so grim?" And then he zeroed in on Tiana. Not hampered by Odin's need to ask permission, the dragon snatched Tiana between his forelegs and drilled into her mind. The flicker and flare of his magic crackled between them.

She writhed in his grip. "Put me down."

Nidhogg ignored her struggles. They must have been laughable to him. Still holding her, his whirling eyes sought mine. Questions roiled through me. I didn't ask a one. The dragon would seal my fears in his own time.

"She must come to Fire Mountain," he growled.

"Why?" Abria made a grab for Tiana but couldn't reach her.

"Leviathans added their essence to hers. Raphael did too. I can erase dragon taint. Not much I can do about what the archangel left."

"Is that why my wings are black?" Tiana asked in tremulous tones.

At least she sounded like herself.

"Aye," the dragon answered.

"Why Fire Mountain?" Abria repeated. "Anything you can do there, you could accomplish here."

Nidhogg lowered Tiana into Abria's arms. "Because only

time will tell if she can move beyond Raphael's branding. She is safer with dragonkind."

For once, the dragon meant well, but Tiana would never leave my watchful eye. Not until her spirit was healed. I quested about for a diplomatic way to get my point across.

Avian screeches and wingbeats snatched my attention skyward.

Griffons flew our way. At least a dozen. Their plumage varied from light to deep brown. Their hides were lion-gold.

"There they are." Arianrhod looked pleased as she beckoned the mystical creatures to a landing place nearby.

Tiana squirmed out of Abria's arms and ran to the griffons, throwing her arms around one of them. He had to be who'd been with her in the passageway. I hurried over in time to hear her being introduced to the griffon's mate.

"How'd you know to come?" Tiana asked, her gaunt face wreathed in smiles.

"I invited them," Arianrhod told her. "As a surprise for you. It's the least I could do for not keeping a closer eye on you in the first place."

Tiana turned to her friend's mate. "Were you as dumb as me?" she asked.

I cringed. This was not the way to treat such majestic beasts.

"What do you mean, little one?" the griffon asked.

"I ate and drank when Raphael offered it, and now he"—Tiana pointed at Nidhogg—"says I'm lost maybe forever."

Several sets of griffon beaks clacked noisily. "It wasn't dumb," the female griffon said firmly. "It was survival. And yes, I took food from that bastard."

"We can carve out the evil," the griffon's mate said. "My kin figured out how to do that once Crine returned home without me."

"We appreciate it"—Abria had reached us—"but let's not be hasty. What worked for griffons might not work for my daughter."

"We're manipulating magic, not protoplasm," the griffon assured her. Bending, he brushed his beak over Abria's cheek. "Your daughter freed me. I would never harm her."

"What happens if we do nothing?" Abria asked.

No one seemed willing to answer my mate, so I did. "It's a crapshoot," I told her. "Tiana may well fight off the tracks Raphael laid within her. Or she might succumb to them. If that happens, we will lose her forever."

Tiana's face, already pale, turned dead white. She swayed on her feet.

I shouldn't have been so blunt, but there's no way to sugarcoat some things.

"This must be done in order," Nidhogg trumpeted. "My task is first. Once I finish, the young mage can receive whatever interventions the griffons deem necessary."

At least he'd moved away from swooping her off to Fire Mountain.

"No." Abria planted both feet in front of the dragon. "I will bring her home. If we cannot repair the damage, then I'll consider your offer."

Nidhogg blew smoke in her face. "Do not be a fool, animal mage. By then, 'twill be too late. I can already see the poison spreading."

His words forced me to scan Tiana with magic of my own. It took a couple of passes, but then I saw the same thing. A darkness expanding from her magical center outward.

Abria batted smoke aside. "I'll call on the ley lines," she insisted. "They'll help me."

Tiana turned to her mother. "I want the dragon and griffons to heal me," she said.

"You don't know what you're requesting," Abria said sternly.

"I love you," our daughter said, "but once the dragon mentioned poison, everything made sense. It's why I feel so bad, so off kilter. Why my wings are still growing darker, and why I look twenty years older."

I made my way to Abria. "We have to trust them."

"You should listen," Arianrhod spoke up. "There are no coincidences. When I searched out the griffon nest to invite them to today's festivities, I had no idea why I put in the effort, but it seemed like the right thing to do."

Abria stilled; light pulsed around her as she consulted the lines. At least I assumed it was what she was doing since when she communed with them she took on a glowing aspect.

Finally, she nodded. "I do not like this," she said. "If any harm befalls my daughter, you will answer to me."

She fell silent. Hedrek fluttered to her shoulder. "It will be all right," he murmured.

"How can you know?" She stroked his feathers.

"Because I trust the dragons, and so should you."

Tiana walked to Nidhogg. "I am ready."

"You request this of your own free will?" the dragon intoned. "Fair warning; it will not be pleasant."

"Neither is being turned to evil. Yes. Please help me."

Pride in my daughter swelled through me. Despite her youth, she was making decisions mages twice her age would have struggled with.

"We shall return," Nidhogg announced. In a flash of fiery light, he and Tiana vanished.

"What if she never comes back?" Abria demanded.

"Have a little faith, child," Arianrhod counseled.

Abria shot her a pained look.

Hedrek hooted, offering the owl version of comfort.

I was more worried about Nidhogg misjudging, treating Tiana more like a young dragon, and injuring her, but I didn't voice my fears. "Tiana requested this," I reminded Abria.

"So she did." My mate shook her head. "We just got her back. I couldn't stand it if we lost her again."

"We won't," I said firmly and hoped to every god in the universe I was right.

Mages and Valkyries swirled around us. I didn't feel like drinking or eating, so I didn't. Neither did Abria.

An hour passed, and then one more.

Finally, when Abria was strung so tight I feared she'd burst, blaming everyone in range for losing her child, Nidhogg dropped out of the sky with Tiana on his back.

Her wings were shading back to their normal green. She spread them to break her fall as she jumped down.

Hedrek, who'd never left Abria's shoulder, launched into

the air hooting excitedly as if to say, "I told you everything would work out."

"Took longer than I expected," Nidhogg explained. "The Leviathans were sneaky. I had to take care to extract what they inserted leaving everything else intact."

I expected Tiana to come to us. Instead, she ran to the griffons. "I feel so much better already," she told them.

"We'll finish the job," her griffon friend assured her.

I bowed to the Norse dragon. "Thank you. We are deeply grateful for your intercession."

Abria bowed too. "Apologies for doubting you. If you would still like me as a guest in Fire Mountain, I will come willingly."

This time, he breathed steam over her. "We might take you up on that, animal mage."

The griffons' healing was much quicker. I couldn't see what they did since it transpired behind a barrier. When it fell, Tiana stood tall. I scanned her to make certain no taint remained, holding my breath until I was done.

"Look!" Abria pointed at our daughter's spread wings.

Instead of black and green, they'd added brown and golden feathers to the mix. I hurried to the griffon who'd befriended Tiana. "You are welcome in Underhill. If ever you have need of a boon, I will turn the world upside down to provide it."

"You are most welcome, Sidhe," the griffon cawed. "We have become insular since we fell from sight. This day's events are an omen. We are no longer alone."

"Can we finally have the party now?" Odin's booming voice filled Asgard's golden streets.

Abria was hugging Tiana. I wrapped my arms and wings around them both.

Above us, Valkyries sang, their voices beautiful as they harmonized. The frothy brew flowed freely. I left Abria and Tiana at a long table in places of honor at its head while I shook hands and visited with mages I hadn't seen in years. Griffons weren't the only ones who'd grown insular.

Tiana didn't know it, but thanks to her, a new age of magic was dawning, one where we'd work together to keep our craft alive in every world.

Later, much later, I'd gather my family and go home. For now, we were exactly where we belonged. A Valkyrie dropped another mug into my outstretched hand. Raising it, I toasted her and her sisters.

"Good to be valued." She grinned, spread her silver wings, and flew on.

CHAPTER 19
EPILOGUE, TIANA

Many years have passed since my fall from grace. Hard as it is for me to say, everything that happened was necessary. Nothing less dramatic would have pounded reality into my head.

Or gotten my attention.

I made my peace with Kirwan and Breanne. Of course, neither trusted my change of heart for a while. I didn't hold it against them. I'd been worse than horrid. Not that I didn't have the occasional moment when the old highhanded me made a cameo appearance.

I quashed that side damned quick. She'd gotten me into serious trouble.

I may actually end up queen of the Sidhe someday, but not for a very long while. I have much to learn, but I'm working hard. Every day brings me closer to the role I was born into.

A role I've come to value and welcome. The old me

thought the whole queen thing was stupid; the new me is much wiser. Sidhe magic is ancient, a tradition I'm proud to be part of.

Sometimes I hurt where the dragon carved bits and pieces out of me. He wasn't gentle, but he was thorough. If I never see another Leviathan, it will be too soon. It's not likely since they're imprisoned somewhere beyond Fire Mountain. Nidhogg says they can't ever escape.

I hope he's right.

Raphael is another story. He'll come for me someday, but I can't think about it. All I can do is hone my magic so I have a prayer of being ready when the day comes.

Momma and I visit the griffons every month or so. I suppose I'm part griffon now since my wings look something like theirs. But magic is magic, and I'm not complaining. At least my feathers are prettier than they used to be.

And there's a young griffon I really like spending time with. We're too young to do much in the way of planning, but my heart skips into hyperdrive whenever I see him.

Auntie Arianrhod says there are no coincidences. Whatever drove me out of the pit in search of an escape hatch saved my life. It also kicked the door open for me to meet Kiern

Oops. I wasn't supposed to say his name out loud. Forget you heard it please. The griffons are superstitious about many things, and keeping their true names hidden is one of them.

Momma is calling. Means it's time to go. Tonight is a full moon, and we'll be riding unicorns to join up with several packs of wolves. Hedrek is coming. So is Cailleach.

I am so blessed. Momma is amazing. Father is just and wise. They've long since forgiven me for my youthful indiscretions.

Hold your dear ones close. Magic is all around you. All you need to do is open your eyes to the wonder, and it will snatch you into its arms.

Until next time, dear readers. Many thanks for sharing my journey.

Love and light to all, Tiana.

You've reached the end of *Tiana*, and the Wayward Mage books. I do hope you've enjoyed them. While you're thinking about it, please leave a review for *Tiana* while it's fresh in your mind. Reviews mean so much to authors. It's a way for you to let other readers know what you loved about a book.

If you enjoyed this series, you might like my Magick and Misfits books. A sample from *Court of Rogues* follows.

BOOK DESCRIPTION, COURT OF ROGUES

Urban fantasy and slow burn romance wrapped into a serial that will keep you up reading long into the night.

Strange bedfellows rock worlds.

Reluctant recruit to the nines, I became Faery's regent by default. Sure, I was next in line for the throne, but I never believed Oberon and Titania were gone for good until first a decade rolled by, and then two, and then ten.

They'll never be back, and the land is mourning. Or pissed. It's hard to tell which, and I'm not sure what difference it makes. I split my time between Faery and Earth searching for a way to mend the rift that's killing my realm. I haven't made much progress. Time is running through the glass, mocking my paltry efforts.

A sultry Witch is barely a blip on the radar. So what if she counts cards in the casino I run on Earth and makes my pit boss a little nuts? Out of the blue, she spits out the unbelievable, and I discover she's not a Witch after all. A glamour hid her Fae-Sidhe blood so well, she'd fooled me.

Her mixed blood is an affront. By rights, I should haul her before the Court to face justice. She understood the chance she took revealing herself to me, and her offer to join forces is tempting, but it could cost me my throne.

Some risks are worth the price. If I cross the line, there'll be no going back.

CHAPTER ONE, CYN

The door to my cramped office slapped against its stops, rattling the frosted glass blazoned with Jedediah Rolfson, General Manager, Lady Luck Casino. The gilt lettering had faded, but everyone in the gaming house knew who I was and where to find me. Of course, Jedediah isn't my true name. Names hold immeasurable power. Even if mortals had been able to pronounce my real one, I'd never, never give them that sort of leverage over me.

My door was still vibrating. A knock would have been nice. Respectful, even, but manners had passed most mortals by. Fueled by irritation, my power simmered so close to the surface it took an effort to rein it in. No need to turn around to identify the man who'd disturbed what passed for peace in this place.

"What is it, Rudy?" I still hadn't swiveled my chair to face him.

"How'd you know it was me?" he demanded.

Because I can smell you, idiot...

I did twist then. The motion of my big body forced the ratty leather chair around almost as an afterthought. Stick-straight black hair fell across Rudy's face, and his white shirt was rolled to the elbows. His usual dark pants were rucked up over the tops of battered leather boots. He looked more like a kitchen knave than a pit boss—an underfed kitchen knave who'd stopped growing as a teenager. I made a point of hiring oddballs—freaks and losers. They weren't in a rush to use Lady Luck as a steppingstone for something better.

Angling a pointed look his way, I growled, "Never mind how I know things. What's gone wrong?" I snapped my fingers in the vain hope he might hurry things up.

He squeezed his bloodshot dark eyes shut for a count of two before opening them. "That infernal twit who counts cards is back."

Many patrons count cards, but only one had posed a challenge recently. Interest flickered as I constructed an image of the leggy red-haired Witch with an iridescent nimbus of power floating around her. "You mean the woman?"

"Of course I mean the blasted woman." A touch of his Russian accent slipped through. "She's the only one who's been able to beat our system."

"What exactly were you hoping I'd do?"

Color stained his sallow cheeks. It was such an unusual response, I delved into his mind and helped myself to his thoughts. Mortals were quite the superficial lot. Culling through their secrets saved me a lot of time.

"Well?" I snapped my fingers again, more out of frustration than actual hope it would move Rudy off the dime.

"Maybe you can tell her to leave." He drew himself up to his full five-foot-eight-inch height, but it didn't have the desired effect. He wanted me to respect him, to back his play, but I'd seen the whole sorry charade in his puny mind. He'd chased the Witch out the last time she stopped by the casino, but he'd also done his damnedest to fuck her.

She'd lured him with a fine set of tits, and then hexed him. Even though he had no concept of what she'd done, her sneaky spell had rendered him impotent. I smothered a chuckle. Witchy charms had a shelf-life. Eventually his little johnny would stand up and salute again, and—

A muted crash came through the audio on one of many screens I'd had mounted so I could see the entire gaming house. Not that I needed them, but they looked good and avoided explanations about how I knew jack concerning the brawl in the basement lounge. The patrons had no idea I spied on them—until I turned them over to the authorities for cheating the house. I've been called a lot of names since I was suckered into taking on this thankless job. So far, I've maintained my cool.

Eventually, though, some hapless mortal will find himself skewered by Fae magic. They'll beg for mercy, for the compassion of a human court, but it will be too late. Mortals never leave Faery unless we release them, not intact, anyway. Those who break free end up in institutions.

"Jed?" Rudy prodded.

"Yeah. Yeah. On my way." I flowed out of my seat. If Rudy weren't hovering in my doorway, I'd have teleported four floors down. Meanwhile, the ruckus was escalating amid the crash of breaking glassware.

"The thieving card counter?" Rudy's gaze skittered away.

"Is that why you're still standing there?" I made shooing motions with both hands. "Christ. Strap on a set. Get moving. I have bigger problems."

The color that had stained his face turned an ugly tomato shade before he spun and pelted down a nearby stairwell mumbling in Russian. He thought I'd never hear him, but he was whining about the fight that had broken out not being on his floor. If it were, the Witch would have beat a hasty retreat.

A snarl of frustration burbled past my throat. I'd never been able to pound the whole team player concept down everyone's throats. Rudy had risen to pit boss because he was honest—and loyal. Maybe it was too much to expect him—or any human in my employ—to show any initiative beyond the basics.

He didn't like me, but then none of the staff did. They sensed I was different, couldn't put their fingers on why that was, and felt uncomfortable in my presence.

Good. I'd never lift a finger to alter their instinctive dread of me.

The day humans can lounge in front of Fae royalty— never mind how far we've fallen—is the day for me to retire to the *Dreaming* and never resurface. A quick glance at the monitor reassured me the brawl was in full swing. No one would notice an unorthodox entrance, so I hopped on an enchanted conduit and emerged in the largest of five gaming halls in a blaze of light.

Muted light, but it still would have given someone pause. Not here, though, and not now. What looked like a motorcycle gang—leather and tatts and piercings—had faced off against a bunch of Asian street hoods who fancied themselves a modern-day version of the mob.

Ha! Bugsy and Al, two of my old buddies, would have laughed until they puked at the comparison. They'd understood how to be badasses because they'd borrowed liberally from Faery. Much of their wickedness never saw the light of day; they were too smart to reveal themselves, and I'd sworn them to silence. Most mortals wouldn't honor such a bond, but they did. They had no idea what I was, but they'd absorbed my lessons like mother's milk. I crossed a few lines —eh, more than a few—by teaching them gruesome ways to inflict pain and death. Even then, my kingdom was on its way out. What were a few more broken rules?

Turned out flaunting Fae law held a price beyond measure, but I'm getting ahead of things.

No one noticed me as I crunched over broken glass, my fury growing at the senseless destruction. The acrid stench of piss merged with the coppery tang of blood. If I didn't establish control over the situation, this room wouldn't be usable for a few days.

Unacceptable. The tables in this gambling hall raked in better than $50,000 a night.

Grunts and curses rained around me as men punched and knifed one another. I sent magic spiraling out, hunting for the telltale bite of metal. Lady Luck had a no-firearms-or-knives rule, and a metal detector sat at the main entrance. It netted us an impressive array of weapons that we stashed in a safe and turned over to the cops once a week.

Yeah. That's right. Bring a gun or a shiv into my club, and you have to petition the cops to get it back. Works great if the piece is legal, but most of them weren't. Ever since I'd established that brilliant bit of policy, we hadn't seized too many of them.

I'd made it to the front of the large hall. Not a dealer or croupier in sight. Either they were hiding in the shadows, or they'd fled at the first hint of trouble. I'd deal with that later. They were supposed to alert someone like Rudy. Or me. I employed half a dozen pit bosses who rotated through the club.

I'd heard from Rudy, but not about this mess.

Someone catapulted into me from the side brandishing a knife. I punched him squarely in the neck, and he dropped like a stone. Shouts told me I'd made someone happy by knocking out one of their enemies. Another dude decked out in black leather rushed me from the back. I knew he was coming, but I let him think he was getting away with something.

I swear, mortals' intelligence has been on the wane for the past hundred years. If Shit For Brains had any at all, he'd have recognized a dead-to-the-world five-year-old would have heard him bearing down on me. Timing is everything. I turned at the precise moment to hit him with a one-two combo to the gut and heart. I might have killed him, but I didn't care.

Once he was squealing and twitching at my feet, I cupped my hands around my mouth and amplified my voice with magic laced with you'd-better-do-what-I-say-or-your-days-will-be-numbered compulsion.

"Stop. Right Now." Three little words. No need to repeat them.

A slow lazy smile formed, stretching my face into an unaccustomed configuration. Yay me. I still had it. Everyone had frozen in place.

"Excellent," I went on, smooth as melted butter. "Everyone get the fuck out of here except your top dogs. Take the fallen with you."

As the crowd cleared, shuffling toward the door, another of my pit bosses scuttled to my side and cleared her throat. "Sorry, boss," Tatiana mumbled. "I went to find you, but your office was empty."

Kind of like your head.

I'd learned to squelch comments like that long ago. Mortals were notoriously thin-skinned, and Tatiana reeked of fear. She hadn't pissed herself, but it had been nip-and-tuck. Her blonde hair was in an updo, and her skin pale under heavy makeup. She would have been pretty without all the war paint. Blue eyes, her best feature, were framed by thick lashes, and she wore Lady Luck's standard employee uniform: white shirt and black pants. Most of the shirts carried the Lady Luck logo, a phoenix sinking into a crater.

The symbolism escaped everyone except me, and I'd never been in a sharing mood when it came to questions like, "What's that mean, boss?" Besides, even if I told them it represented Faery's decline, they'd have thought I'd had too much to drink.

Meanwhile, four men had moved closer, but not too close. Like I said, I make humans nervous.

"Yeah?" One narrowed his eyes. "What'd you want us for?"

I nailed him with my gaze. I employ a glamour. It smooths the points of my ears and makes my eyes appear blue, rather than a mix of silver and gold with coppery centers. For the slightest of moments, I let it slip a notch, just a hint of a blur.

The dude rubbed his eyes. "Shit. Drunker than I thought." His words were slurred.

It was tempting to display more of what I really was. I shrugged it off. No point in making him yearn for the impossible. He'd be drawn to my deviant beauty. More than drawn. He'd twist himself into a pretzel for one more peek. If I'd wanted a lackey, sure, but I had other plans for him and his partners in crime.

"You have two choices," I told the men who were shifting from foot to foot as they looked mostly at the floor. "Grab mops and buckets and clean up the mess you made."

"Or?" One tried for a sneer, but didn't quite manage it.

"Or I hold you here and call the cops. Property damage is a felony. Bet you've had a few of those already."

I rocked back on my heels, waiting. Tatiana had drawn closer to me, not because I was warm and fuzzy, but because the thugs made her even more nervous than I did.

"Big talk. How are you planning to keep us from leaving?" Shit For Brains Number Two asked.

I swept an arm wide. "I don't have to. You're all on camera. I give the cops the feed and voila." I dusted my hands together. "I'm sure they know you already."

"We'll clean," he gritted out.

"It would go faster with more of us," another pointed out.

"Probably so, but I don't want 'more of you' in here," I told him. "While we're on that little topic, you and your gang members are barred from Lady Luck from here on in."

The one who'd said his life would be simpler with drones to order about drew himself up. "You can't do that, man."

"The hell I can't," I retorted and turned to Tatiana. "Show these fellows where the cleaning supplies are and oversee the work. They don't leave until you're satisfied they've done a good job."

Her blue eyes widened. "Erm. Maybe the head of janitorial would be better for that."

"He might be," I agreed, trying for an amiable tone, "but I assigned this job to you."

Something in my voice told her arguing was pointless. She'd run at the first whiff of fighting. That story about coming to find me had been pure fabrication. She rolled her shoulders back, barked, "Follow me," and loped across the expanse of parquet flooring.

After a pause a shade too long for my liking, the men turned to follow her. Just so there'd be no misunderstandings later, I called after them, "Don't even think about hassling her. If you do, I'll find out."

I left it there. No need to spell out what I'd do to their

sorry, shitty asses if they made a grab for Tatiana's tits or any other part of her. I retreated to one side and wrapped myself in shadows. I wouldn't remain long, only until the cleanup project was underway.

I hadn't realized I'd clenched my hands into fists, and I uncurled my fingers one by one. Damn it, anyway. Everything was broken—and I didn't mean in this gaming room. I was here, straddling worlds, to mend what I could, but I hadn't made much progress.

Or any if I were honest.

Aye, and when I start lying to myself, I'm done for, a patronizing inner voice spouted off.

I wasn't the source of the original damage. It could be traced directly to the Fae court, who'd decided it would be a grand idea to kick Faery's gates open to mortals a century ago. Not that any of us ever cared about humans. We've always held them in contempt, but we wanted their money.

They'd done a bang-up job stripping their world of everything salable and grown filthy rich in the process. My kinsmen are drawn by gold—and I'd be lying if I said it didn't sing to me as well. We all love wealth, which is strange since our creature needs are taken care of in Faery.

At first, around the end of the 1800s, everything appeared to be going smoothly. We provided something not unlike a circus attraction for the well-heeled. One element none of us had reckoned on was Faery herself. Our land is alive, and she rebelled at the presence of those without power. Not right away, but when it happened the backlash was swift, sure, and brutal...

Buckets clattered as they rolled across the faux wooden

floor. Some establishments have carpet. Not mine. For just this reason. My impromptu work crew dug in. Two men looked as if they'd never seen a mop before, but after Tatiana taunted them for being inept dicks, they shaped up.

I heard cheers from the strip show one floor up. No reason for me to stay here. I'd have it out with the dealers and croupiers at the all-staff meeting tomorrow afternoon. Tucking my hands into my pockets, I strolled through a wall, angling until I intersected a stairwell. Rather than naming the deserters, perhaps I'd be better served reiterating club policies to everyone.

The more I considered it, the better I liked my idea. I'd gin up something and have everyone e-sign it. I started to head for the floor show. Getting a gander at bouncing breasts and shaved pussies always settled my mind. Or diverted it, anyway. My cock thickened where it was tucked into my trousers, and I curled my fingers around it, enjoying sensation as it skittered through me.

Sex served as a reminder of the Witch. My cock grew more distended as I remembered her striking face and generous curves. To hell with the dancers in the lounge. I wanted the Witch—up close and personal.

If she was still in Lady Luck, I'd weave a lust spell, make her see only me. My errant member twitched against my fingers. "Yes, yes," I told my sidekick. "She'll want you so much, she won't be able to contain herself."

Rudy managed the blackjack and poker tables. A magnet for card counters, they spanned two rooms on the second floor. I couldn't do much about my erection. It would be as useless as attempting to stuff a genie back into a bottle, so I crafted a diversion spell from my waist down. It would draw eyes away from the tented-out front of my pants.

I bounded into the nearest chamber, gratified by the small noises that verified Lady Luck was making money. Chips clicking, dealers calling for bets, and cries of delight as patrons raked in cash.

Rudy sidled up to me. "How'd it go?"

"It's handled. How about your assignment."

He screwed his face into an angry mask, adding ten years to his grizzled appearance. "I tried, but I'm not getting anywhere near that bitch ever again. She did something to her blackjack dealer."

"What do you mean, did something?" I added a jot of magical coercion to my question.

"He's not right. Won't look at me. Won't answer me."

Damn my eyes, it sure sounded like a hex. "Is she still at his table?"

Rudy nodded. "I told the dealer not to authorize payout, but—"

"Never mind. I'll take it from here."

"Thanks." For once, Rudy looked cowed, and embarrassed. Like most men, admitting defeat is right up there with swallowing glass shards.

The Witch wasn't in this room, so I crossed the hall and walked into the other one. The feel of her power smacked me mid-chest. Witch magic smells delightful. Aged whiskey and wildflowers with a touch of blood to blend everything together. This witch was old. I could tell from her scent and the extent of her power. It oozed from her and had wrapped around the dealer in visible strands.

Oberon's balls. She didn't need to count cards. She had the dealer in thrall. What did she think she was? A fucking Vampire? Whatever game she was running, she could damn well take it elsewhere.

I strode across the big room with its colorful tables. Horse races played on big screen televisions lining one wall. We took a bite out of bets placed on them too. Unlike a mortal, the Witch knew I was coming. I felt her attention, even though her back was turned.

A long skirt swirled around her sandal-clad feet. Made of a pale green sheer material, it offered tantalizing glances of long legs and made it clear she hadn't bothered with under-wear. An equally sheer tunic made of silver fabric embroidered with violet runes covered her from shoulder to hip. Her shapely arms were bare. She told the dealer to hold up —in Gaelic—and he complied. I knew damn good and well Hector didn't speak Gaelic. He's Native American from a local reservation.

How deep in trance did she have him, anyway, that he responded to commands in a foreign tongue?

Slowly, tantalizingly, she twisted until she faced me, upper body first, followed by a two-step motion that bought her hips around. Her eyes were a pale, clear green, her face a study in perfection with high, slanted cheekbones, a regal forehead, and a strong chin.

When she smiled and ran her tongue over her lush lower lip, I dropped a hasty ward around myself. She could dupe a mortal—snare them in her spells—but I was Fae, and my interest in fucking her had staged a dramatic retreat.

The Witch angled her head to one side, still giving me come-hither vibes. "I know what you are," she purred.

Her words tossed still more cold water on my arousal. "Aye, and I know what ye are as well, Madame Witch," I growled back in Gaelic. "Get out of my casino."

Her full lips formed a pout. "You're no fun." Her magic intensified, pummeling my warding.

My control snapped and I grabbed her upper arm, squeezing hard. "Where is your coven? I will return you, as is my duty for any renegade Witch." I'd stuck to Gaelic, and an archaic form at that. Zero chance of anyone understanding it—other than Witchy-gal.

"No need to get tetchy." She yanked her arm, but I held fast.

"Your coven?" I added a whopping heap of compulsion to my query.

Her face twisted in pain, and I had a momentary twinge of conscience for forcing her. "Don't have one," she ground out.

Her reply had been true, but it shocked me. "Covens are a requirement," I lectured. "After the Witch uprising of 1943—"

A violent twist jerked her arm out of my grasp. "Don't lecture me on my own history," she hissed. "I'm...different."

"We all are, sweetheart," I told her tartly. "Misfits attract magic."

Her lips twitched into half a smile. "Hate to admit it, but that's catchy."

Fuckity-fuck. She was still trying to con me. "Yeah. Now beat it. And don't come back."

"But I need the money." Her pouty look was back.

"Not my problem, darling. Turn tricks. Get an honest job. Before you go, release my dealer from whatever you did to him."

"If I do, will you hire me?"

The question came out of left field, leaving me dumbstruck. Luckily, a loss for words never lasts long. I started to say hell would freeze over before I'd offer her work, but something stayed my tongue.

"Show up here at five tomorrow afternoon. We'll talk about it."

She tilted her chin and ran her gaze from my toes to my head. Something about her direct stare got me going all over again, even through my warding.

"Good enough." She nodded and walked to the dealer. Reaching into his pants pocket, she withdrew a charm, breathed on it, and we both watched it disintegrate into motes of light.

I eyed the dealer. He still stood motionless, a dreamy expression in place. "Get rid of the other ones too," I told her.

Breath swooshed from her mouth. "I was getting to them. Can't hurry these things or he might turn into the village idiot."

Village idiots predated medieval times, so I asked, "How old are you?"

"Never ask a lady her age," she retorted and retrieved two more charms. By the time they were dead, the dealer was starting to look more like a man and less like a puppet.

She regarded him and spoke a few words before turning

to me. "There. Give it a few and he won't remember a thing about any of this. See you tomorrow." Her hips swung enticingly as she strode away.

"What's your name?" I called after her.

"You'll find out tomorrow. When I complete the employment application," she replied in mind speech, not bothering to turn around.

I was still sorting how a Witch had mastered telepathy, not a skill native to their magic, when the dealer made a grunting noise. "Boss. What happened? I feel...off."

"Take a break," I told him. "Back to your table in fifteen."

Without waiting for more questions, I walked out of the card room. It was only an hour from closing time. I could skip the rest of tonight's never-ending drama and slip into Faery. My magic needed a boost, and my mind a rest. The mortal world dragged at me, drained my essence, and made me long for an earlier time.

One before we'd opened our doors to humankind.

Keep right on reading. Click here.

ABOUT THE AUTHOR

Ann Gimpel is a USA Today bestselling author. A lifelong aficionado of the unusual, she began writing speculative fiction a few years ago. Since then her short fiction has appeared in many webzines and anthologies. Her longer books run the gamut from urban fantasy to paranormal romance. Once upon a time, she nurtured clients. Now she nurtures dark, gritty fantasy stories that push hard against reality. When she's not writing, she's in the backcountry getting down and dirty with her camera. She's published over 100 books to date, with several more planned for 2023 and beyond. A husband, grown children, grandchildren, and wolf hybrids round out her family.

Keep up with her at www.anngimpel.com or http://anngimpel.blogspot.com

If you enjoyed what you read, get in line for special offers and pre-release special reads. Newsletter Signup!

ALSO BY ANN GIMPEL

Kylian

Grigori

Magick and Misfits

Court of Rogues

Midnight Court

Court of the Fallen

Court of Destiny

Coven Enforcers

Blood and Magic

Blood and Sorcery

Blood and Illusion

Demon Assassins

Witch's Bounty

Witch's Bane

Witches Rule

Dragon Heir

Dragon's Call

Dragon's Blood

Dragon's Heir

Dragon Lore

Highland Secrets

To Love a Highland Dragon

Dragon Maid

Dragon's Dare

Dragon Fury

Earth Reclaimed

Earth's Requiem

Earth's Blood

Earth's Hope

Elemental Witch

Timespell

Time's Curse

Time's Hostage

Gatekeeper

Shadow Reaper

Rebel Reaper

Untamed Reaper

GenTech Rebellion

Winning Glory

Honor Bound

Claiming Charity

Loving Hope

Keeping Faith

Ice Dragon

Feral Ice

Cursed Ice

Primal Ice

Magick and Misfits

Court of Rogues

Midnight Court

Court of the Fallen

Court of Destiny

Rubicon International

Garen

Lars

Soul Dance

Tarnished Beginnings

Tarnished Legacy

Tarnished Prophecy

Tarnished Journey

Soul Storm

Dark Prophecy

Dark Pursuit

Dark Promise

Underground Heat

Roman's Gold

Wolf Born

Blood Bond

Wayward Mage

Hands of Fate

Jinxed

Hunted

Salvaged

Tiana

Wolf Clan Shifters

Alice's Alphas

Megan's Mates

Sophie's Shifters

Wylde Magick

Gemstone

Lion's Lair

Unbalanced

STANDALONE BOOKS

Branded, That Old Black Magic Romance (paranormal romance)

Edge of Night (short story collection, paranormal and horror)

Grit is a 4-Letter Word (nonfiction)

Heart's Flame (post-apocalyptic romance)

Icy Passage (science fiction romance)

Marked by Fortune (post-apocalyptic coming of age story)

Melis's Gambit (historical paranormal romance)

Midnight Magic (paranormal romance)

Red Dawn (post-apocalyptic paranormal romance)

Shadow Play (historical paranormal romance)

Shadows in Time (Highland time travel romance)

Since We Fell (contemporary romance)

Warin's War (paranormal romance)

www.ingramcontent.com/pod-product-compliance
Lightning Source LLC
Chambersburg PA
CBHW010842190726
48286CB00012BA/2950